NOT SO SURPRISE ENDINGS

Not So Surprise Endings

A collection of short stories

by

SUSAN L. POLLET

Adelaide Books
New York / Lisbon
2021

NOT SO SURPRISE ENDINGS
A collection of short stories
By Susan L. Pollet

Published by Adelaide Books, New York / Lisbon
adelaidebooks.org

Editor-in-Chief
Stevan V. Nikolic

For any information, please address Adelaide Books
at info@adelaidebooks.org
or write to:
Adelaide Books
244 Fifth Ave. Suite D27
New York, NY, 10001

ISBN: 978-1-955196-96-3

Printed in the United States of America

"This is not the end. It is not even the beginning of the end.

But it is, perhaps, the end of the beginning."

—Winston Churchill

I dedicate this book to Amos, who continually inspires me to create, and to Katharine and Eve, who are sublime creations. I further dedicate this book to all those people throughout the world who lost their lives as a result of the coronavirus pandemic.

Contents

Prologue

This is a collection of stories which explore how, why and what happens when certain things end. The endings sometimes seem predictable from the beginnings and middles, but there are times where the endings surprise one. What occurs after the ending, if anything? What happens to the pastor who speaks ill of his dead wife? What does paradise turn into when it becomes something else? When do you know certain relationships are over? What does an obsession with youth produce? What does rudeness lead to? What happens when a Queen Bee misuses her power and stings? Can a person obsessed with perfectionism overcome it? Does your dog become a person to you, and how does that play out? Where does being selfish lead to? Who can a spoiled child turn into as an adult? When someone dies, do men and women grieve differently and does that matter in the end?

While these questions are not necessarily interrelated, the common bond is that there are often consequences resulting from our behaviors, and the actions of others, which can lead to surprising, and not so surprising endings. Perhaps after reading my endings, you will create your own in your mind based on people you have known and the events you have observed as to these topic areas. One thing is certain – not everybody gets what they deserve.

Chapter One

Don't Speak Ill of the Dead

De mortuis nihil nisi bonum dicendum est, a Latin phrase, which loosely translates to "do not speak ill of the dead," is something I read, something I was taught, something I had come to believe was the appropriate way to behave. There was a "good girl" in me who wanted to be ethical and kind towards others at all times, if I could figure out how to do it without losing me in it. But there was another part of my psyche which always questioned beliefs, rules, and laws. What if the person who died had committed a murder, or sexually abused a child, or stole money in a Ponzi scheme and bankrupted large numbers of people? What about a person who committed adultery, emotionally or physically. Should we refuse to speak ill of those persons when they died? Did it protect perpetrators to fail to speak about them? For me, it was always a painful parsing of where the line should be drawn. Perhaps that is your experience too?

An additional layer of what it took to be "good," which is tangentially related, was an edict from my grandmother. She taught me that I should not gossip about others. She was referring to the live ones. She told me that intelligent people had more interesting things to talk about. Again, my mind ran to when it might be appropriate, and even "good" to gossip. Another layer is that one is not supposed to be judgmental. We are taught, "Judge not, that you be not judged." If I judge without rushing and with reason, am I still being judgmental? Am I merely observing? You can see just a few of the reasons why being "good" can be so complicated.

A particular circumstance, involving all of these concepts and which was more nuanced than the usual "fall from grace," has been occupying my dreams. It involved the pastor of our church in a wealthy suburban town in the United States. I will not provide more details about the location so as to protect the privacy of the families involved. Everything I will tell you is second-hand information I heard from other church members. In that sense it was gossip. It was unsubstantiated. Nonetheless, his story created an ethical conundrum for all who heard versions of it.

I was a young mother and wife in the 1990's. I taught in the Sunday school at our church, as did my husband. We were active congregants, and our children were part of the church community. The pastor led our church for twenty years. He was well respected as an intellectual in wider church circles, including internationally. His texts, sermons, and articles on religious matters were frequently quoted.

While I respected him as a scholar, and a hard worker, I could never quite warm up to him. His posture was stiff, his manners were overly formal, his speech was stilted, and he lacked the ability to comfort because of his cold presence. I could not relate to his sermons which had a lot of references that a non-scholar would not know. They seemed to be burdened by the oral equivalent of too many footnotes. Perhaps he was an introvert who had a difficult time connecting with people, which was an odd quality for a pastor. Maybe he thought he was better than everybody else because of his academic prowess, and did not have to make his words relatable. Perhaps he was "better" and the congregation needed to become more erudite. In any event, he showed little emotion, which made it hard to find his humanity.

As with every coin, there is a flip side. The pastor had a wife and three adult children. They lived in a compound. It contained a large, stately home in which he resided with his wife. It had been owned by his wife's family for decades. The compound contained several additional homes for the adult children to reside in with their families, which they did. The pastor and his wife were childhood sweethearts, and their families were close. From an early age, it was determined that they would marry. They were both good looking, smart, and had the proper education for their social class. Her family had money from the bank they owned in the community and their real estate holdings. He was looked upon as a rising star because of his superior intellect. When they married and had children, the community rejoiced. They seemed to be the perfect couple and family. When he finished his studies and became pastor, the circle was complete.

His wife and children attended church services regularly, and were active members of the congregation throughout the years. His wife was a professor of literature at a local college, and was well known in academic circles. When she was in her early fifties, she was diagnosed with Multiple Sclerosis, or MS, which is a chronic illness of the central nervous system. She suffered from that disease for a long time, which eventually severely affected her spinal cord. I do not know the extent to which the MS had impacted upon all parts of her brain, but she retired early. She had been in a wheelchair for a number of years, and, as the story was told, the pastor took care of her with great dedication and perseverance. Perhaps his reserve was the result of a preoccupation with tending to her needs and with keeping himself from falling apart.

The pastor was popular with the older congregants. That popularity grew over the years because of the perception that he was a righteous man who took care of his wife in a loving manner, "in sickness and in health." Additionally, the elders wanted to be part of a prestigious church, and he provided that with his renown. He had an inner circle of leaders within the church who helped him to achieve his goals, and whom he trusted and confided in.

After a prolonged period of treatments, hospitalizations, and painful decline, his wife passed away. She could no longer swallow at the end, and had wasted away to eighty pounds on a five-foot, eight-inch frame. We were told that the pastor remained devoted to her, as he always had, throughout that final period. His profound grief was evident to all in the way he held his body, and in the way he spoke. Everyone wanted to console him and his adult children and grandchildren. The members of the church community wrapped their arms around them.

His wife was buried in the cemetery next to the church where her family members and the pastor's family members were interred. There were plots designated and waiting for the pastor, his children and grandchildren for when the time would come. There was a graveside service for his wife which I attended. The pastor gave a heartfelt eulogy which brought tears to the eyes of all who heard it. He brought emotion to his speech in a manner I had never seen him exhibit before. He told us only the most positive things about his wife, in accordance with his excellent opinion of her, his diplomacy, and the teaching to not speak ill of the dead. Their eldest adult child gave a beautiful speech as well on behalf of the children and grandchildren.

Some time after the funeral, which was widely attended, and written about in the local newspaper and covered on local television, the pastor began to sort through papers and other personal belongings of his wife. She had given him her password to her computer a year prior, but he never used it. After she became wheelchair bound, she did a lot of writing on her computer. She wrote children's stories for her grandchildren, and occupied herself with email to keep in touch with people since her ability to get out of the house was impaired. She stopped handling her own finances at a certain point, and he thought there was a slight possibility that some financial information was sent to her alone via email.

Immediately after her death, he went into her computer to make certain that there was nothing of import there, and perhaps to uncover some writings of hers his children would want to see and cherish. According to the gossip, he was shocked and dismayed by what he found. For a time, he kept the information to himself and did not discuss it with his children.

Within days of the funeral, many eligible widows and divorcees in the congregation began to leave him homemade casseroles at his doorstep with notes of sympathy. The more aggressive ones began to ask him to go out with them to, in their words, keep him company and to prevent his loneliness. He told them that he was not ready to accept their overtures, but thanked them for their kindness.

Notwithstanding his decline of their invitations, and soon after the funeral, people in the congregation observed him at local restaurants, at the movies, and at other venues with a woman who was about twenty years his junior. At that time he was in his late sixties. She was a member of the congregation. She was divorced, dressed in sexy, provocative clothing, bleached her hair the color of Marilyn Monroe's, and wore heavy makeup and expensive jewelry. She was a successful real estate broker in town, seemed to know everybody, and had an outgoing personality. She was the polar opposite of his wife, who, up until her last breath, wore conservative, tailored clothing, little makeup, sensible heirloom jewelry, and was intellectually oriented, quiet and demure.

People began to gossip about these sightings of the pastor and his "girlfriend." There was a lot of discussion about it amongst the members of the congregation. Many judged the pastor harshly. They expressed that his wife was recently buried, and that he should have waited at least one year after she died to start dating. The women whom he rejected complained as well, although they had tried to do the same thing with him and it seemed like "sour grapes" on their part. Some gossiped that he was secretly dating that woman for a few months before his wife died. They said they saw her coming out of his office on frequent occasions at the church prior to the funeral. Others opined that since he had suffered for so many years as a devoted caretaker for his wife, he deserved some pleasure. They argued that people should not make up an artificial timeline for how long one should grieve, and when one should find love at a later age.

There was a group of elder leaders, male and female, who met with the pastor on a regular basis for special dinners to discuss church matters, and to socialize. Three months after the funeral, the pastor attended one of these meetings for the first time since his wife's death.

During the cocktail hour, he had a few glasses of wine, and was uncharacteristically talkative in an animated way. He appeared a "bit unhinged." He took one of the female elders aside. I will call her Madeline, for privacy's sake. She had been a close friend of his wife's for many decades, and was a social worker. He told her that he wanted to discuss something with her, but it was highly confidential. She agreed to come to his office the next day.

The following day, Madeline arrived at his office at the appointed time. He was extremely somber, and asked her to sit down. He was dressed in a black suit, and his face was gray and pinched. He sat behind his desk. She sat in a chair opposite him. According to the gossip, he told Madeline how much he loved his wife, and how grateful he was that he had the strength to care for her lovingly for so many years during her lengthy illness. He asked her to keep what he was about to tell her completely confidential. She agreed. He told Madeline that he thought he could trust her above all.

He communicated to Madeline that in addition to the terrible grief he experienced because of his wife's death, he was simultaneously quite angry with her and felt betrayed. He mentioned, tearfully, that when he accessed his wife's computer after her death, he found multiple emails, going back several years, to and from a close female friend of hers, which he claimed were love letters. He called the woman his wife's "lesbian lover."

He asked Madeline if she knew anything about their relationship. She said that she knew that they were close friends, and loved each other as friends, but that his wife had never expressed to her anything about a lesbian sexual relationship, and they told each other everything. Madeline suggested that perhaps he was reading too much into it. Madeline mentioned that she and his wife often told each other that they loved one another, especially since they realized for a number of years that she was slowly dying. The pastor did not show Madeline the emails, nor did she ask to see them, so she was not certain what they said, or if his interpretation was plausible.

The pastor told Madeline that he had devoted his life to his wife, and apparently her affections were not for him, but for that other woman. He confided that because of his wife's illness, they had not had sexual relations in many years, and that as a man, it was very hard for him. If he had known she did not love him, and was having sex with another, perhaps, he conjectured, he would not have wasted those years on someone who did not reciprocate his feelings. Because his wife's body was so broken, Madeline wondered what he was considering to be sex with her female friend. Was she given some comfort with a massage? Oral sex?

Madeline was afraid to ask.

She did ask him whether he spoke with the "lesbian lover" to confirm or deny that she and his wife had a relationship which was more than friends. The pastor told her that the emails left no doubt of that, and that he could not bring himself to approach that woman further about it. He maintained that it was too humiliating for him.

Madeline became uncomfortable with the direction of the conversation. She told the pastor that hearing him speak ill of her dead close friend was difficult. She begged him not to mention this information to anyone else. She said that even if it were true that his wife had an adulterous, lesbian relationship, which she highly doubted, no good could come from spreading this information now, since she was not alive to defend herself or to explain. Madeline was concerned about the impact of this information on the pastor's adult children, first and foremost, and how their feelings for their father might change if they knew he was telling people these things about their mother. She suggested to him that he might want to seek pastoral counseling for himself, since he had been through so much, and because it was a difficult time for him and his family.

The pastor nodded, and said he would consider her words, but Madeline could see a rising anger in him which frightened her. She was not certain if the anger was because of the "so-called" betrayal. Perhaps he had additional proof in the emails he did not share with her which made it a certainty. Even if his wife did have a lesbian lover, Madeline was convinced, from everything she knew about her dearest friend, that the pastor's wife loved him too and appreciated all that he did for her. Maybe his wife was not in her right mind. Perhaps she wanted to experience everything before she died, and took comfort where she could find it, both physically and mentally.

She surmised that perhaps his anger was a stage of grief, and he was choosing to obsess about and incorrectly interpret those emails as a part of that process. Another possibility she thought about was that maybe he was having an affair with that younger woman everyone was talking about, and he was using these emails to justify his behavior on some level to assuage his guilt.

By the time Madeline left his office, her head was spinning. She had a sense of foreboding. She was not certain what the pastor was going to do next with the information. She hoped he would go for counseling and discuss it in the privacy of that confidential relationship. She went home to her husband, who attended, also, the regular meetings with the pastor at the church and was part of the pastor's inner circle. She remembered that the pastor had asked her to keep their conversation confidential, and was conflicted about mentioning anything about it to her husband.

Madeline and her husband had a special bond. They told each other everything, and were sensitive to subtle changes in one another's moods. Her husband knew that something was upsetting her. It took about five minutes, and mild probing, before she was sharing with him everything the pastor told her. She told him that they had to keep the matter confidential. He agreed that it would be the preferable course.

Meanwhile, the pastor was agitated after his conversation with Madeline. He thought that perhaps because she was a woman, she could not completely understand his point of view.

As a close friend of his wife's, maybe she had a certain bias. He thought that he should share his deep feelings with a close male friend in their inner circle, who might understand things better from a male perspective. He did not consider going to pastoral counseling. He wanted to speak with a friend who knew him well. While the members of the inner circle were a kind of friend, they were truly colleagues who worked together for the sake of the church and the flock. That was a miscalculation on his part.

The next day, the pastor called his male friend whom I will call Matthew for privacy's sake. He made an appointment for Matthew to meet him in his office the following day. When Matthew arrived at the appointed hour, he found the pastor in a state of disarray. It appeared as if the pastor slept in his clothes, his hair was uncombed and dirty, and he had not shaved for several days. The office was a mess with uneaten food on the table and with papers strewn all over the desk and floor. Matthew was disturbed to find their church leader in such a state, especially since he was always so fastidious. The pastor forgot to tell Matthew to keep their conversation confidential as he was so upset. The pastor proceeded to tell Matthew the story about his wife and the emails, and his feelings about it. He cried and cried. Matthew took the pastor's part, and told him that he had every right to be angry with his wife on multiple levels. Matthew told him that he had sacrificed so much for his wife, and that she had sinned. Matthew did not consider that the pastor might need counseling, that he should not speak ill of the dead, or the effect of this information on the pastor's family, friends, and church community.

After Matthew left the pastor's office, he called several other friends in the pastor's inner circle to tell them the pastor's story. By the end of the week, everybody in the congregation knew about it. The gossip escalated the circumstances to a full fledged scandal. Factions began to form. One group wanted the pastor to leave the congregation immediately for speaking ill of his long suffering dead wife. Another group was disgusted with his open relationship with the younger woman so soon after his wife's death and wanted him to leave. They held him to a higher standard.

One group felt sympathetic toward him, and proposed that his exhaustion from his care of his wife, and the shock of the news, caused him to seek comfort by telling friends and colleagues. They determined that he was not trying to shame his dead wife. They argued that this "slip of the tongue" should be excused in light of his excellent scholarship, his long tenure and his good service to the congregation.

It did not take long for his children to hear the story. Unfortunately word reached them from other members of the congregation before their father had a chance to tell them. All three children refused to speak with their father again after hearing the story from him one time. They declined to believe their father's story about their mother. They loved their mother, and thought that his defamation of her reputation was unforgivable. They expressed that even if the story was true, and there was no defamation in the legal sense, his spreading that information was unethical and cruel.

The pain did not end for the pastor. The children were given the compound in their mother's will, which included the home the pastor had lived in with his wife. His children told him that he needed to pack his things and find another place to live immediately. They felt that he should never have told congregation members stories about their mother after she died and could no longer speak to it, even if it were true, which they highly doubted. In addition, they were unhappy with his 'newfound' relationship. Rumor had it that he moved in with his girlfriend. She stopped attending the pastor's church because of ill feelings towards her by other congregants. His children would not permit him to see his grandchildren, and they refused to acknowledge his relationship with his girlfriend.

Many members of his inner circle would no longer meet with him for church meetings.

After a year of being ostracized and talked about, the pastor decided to leave on his own volition, although he was in essence forced to resign. He married the younger woman, retired, and moved to Florida. His children refused to attend the wedding. Word spread throughout the congregation that he was traveling extensively, lecturing internationally, and enjoying his new found freedom.

One year after his retirement, the pastor was visiting Jerusalem with his wife. He was retracing the steps of the Crucifixion of Jesus. While walking the stations of the cross, he started to feel intense chest pains, and experienced nausea and shortness of breath. The tour guide called an ambulance and he was rushed to the hospital, accompanied by his wife. He learned that he had suffered a massive heart attack. Although he was not Catholic, he asked that he be given the "last rites," which appeared to calm him. The next day he passed away. His body was shipped back to the United States. His children would not let him be buried next to their mother. Nobody is certain where his second wife had him buried. Many members of the congregation and his children are still speaking ill of him even though he is dead.

Chapter Two

Escape From Paradise

"Wherever my travels may lead, paradise is where I am."
(Not always).

—Voltaire

The winter was harsh. As we entered our seventieth year, we were living in an apartment in New York City. While we had made our home a comfortable nest, we craved sunlight. We were feeling bone weary, as were so many around us. We decided to celebrate our respective birthdays, in January, by traveling to an island called St. Francis, which was described in all of the tourist advertisements as "paradise on earth." It would be a welcome respite from the snow and ice, and would satisfy our fantasies of idyllic bliss.

Our research about the island revealed that it had long been a playground for the rich and famous. Since we were not in either of those categories, it seemed that a trip there would be akin to entering the Garden of Eden during our lifetime, without fear of the snake. We loved to watch TV shows about fabulous real estate, which was our version of porn. We learned that the island we chose had a French side and a Dutch side, and that it was a matter of crossing an insignificant border from one to the other to experience different cultures. We were not the types to sit on a chair with an umbrella all day on the beach, thus, the idea of experiencing international cuisine, hearing different languages, and learning about new cultures was a decided draw.

We had been to overcrowded third world countries and observed true grinding poverty. This island offered what we thought would be a getaway from all of the burdens on mankind, and on us. In my mind, I pictured virtually empty white sand beaches with shells ripe for the picking, soft tufts of white clouds, gentle water, rock formations, rising hills, verdant landscapes, the smell of flowers in the air, spectacular sunsets, and friendly local people. The power of advertising had invaded my imagination of heaven on earth.

With the turmoil in the world, I felt a slight twinge of guilt that we had the time and the money to celebrate in such a luxurious fashion. On the other hand, we had watched my parents, over a ten-year period, decline into wheelchairs, struggle with dementia, incontinence and a host of illnesses, until their deaths. They died within months of one another, which was a relief to each of them at the time. We wanted to experience all of life's richness while we still could.

Reaching this birthday milestone sent our heads spinning, and into explorer mode. My husband told me that we deserved such a trip and celebration, and I began to believe him.

We were not completely living in a utopia in our heads. While we read that the island, along with many other islands in that sea, had been hit hard by a hurricane several years before, the photographs that we viewed of rental properties did not reflect that damage. There was little current coverage of the situation on the internet. With great optimism and excitement, we rented an apartment high up on a hill, overlooking the sea, on the Dutch part of the island.

Our travel there was uneventful. We did notice, on our drive from the airport to our rental property, that many of the homes and businesses lining the small, pot-holed, bumpy roads were demolished by the hurricane, and had not been re-built. Many of the stores which had been somewhat resurrected, were shabby and looked like bodegas in urban areas. Simultaneously, there was a lot of active construction in gated communities set back from the road. We observed the cranes and heard the unsettling sounds of construction.

It did not appear to be a rich island to me from anyone's point of view, and certainly not from the islanders' perspective. Perhaps it was in the past, but, from what we could observe, the local people who lived on the island year round did not seem to be flourishing. Clearly, tourism was their main industry, but the riches were not being distributed. The gated communities seemed to contain all of the abundance, but they were set back from the road, and accessible only to the privileged. Those communities had suffered damage from the hurricane as well, but it appeared that on the Dutch side, there was an active attempt to restore them.

Our first few days upon arrival were relaxing. The apartment was perfectly situated in a gated community under construction. From our deck, we watched the cruise ships out on the sea, which were of varied size and expense, and noticed the multiple colors of the sea in intricate shades of blue and green which changed with the rotation of the sun. We took long walks in our complex early and late in the day since the midday sun was too strong, and walked down to the seaside restaurant for dinner owned by a French man who had recently rebuilt and reopened the restaurant after the hurricane. He told us that the former restaurant on that exact site had been completely destroyed. He acknowledged that if another hurricane were to strike, his restaurant would be demolished too. Oddly, he did not seem to be concerned. He had a "come what may" attitude. We shopped for food in the local market, and ate several of our meals from our apartment each day. We read, wrote, and meditated. Mostly, we stayed close to our new home.

During one of our early morning walks, a large black flying insect with enormous wings swooped down and stung the soft flesh on my upper inner arm. During that day, and for many days afterward, my arm became red, itchy and extremely swollen. Perhaps because I wore perfume, I was stung by bees and insects many times in the past, or maybe it was the smell my body gave off which made me prone to be the victim. Nonetheless, I felt some sense of foreboding from the intensity of my body's reaction on this occasion. I could not shake the feeling. In my imagination, there were no stinging insects in Shangri-la.

Given our high energy personalities, we grew restless, and similar to Adam and Eve, wanted to explore and learn more. We drove to the French side of the island. Other than a sign at the border, there was not much evidence that we had crossed. The landscape was similar to the Dutch side of the island. The difference was that much more of the devastation of the hurricane was visible, as less was being rebuilt. At that point we did not know why.

In the main town on the French side, where the ferry boats were located, there were a few long, parallel streets with shops that contained all of the luxury goods the cruise people would desire including jewelry, watches and designer clothing. The young employees stood outside of their respective shops and were aggressive with the tourists. They followed them down the street and verbally assaulted them to get them to go into their stores. There was an air of desperation about it which made us uncomfortable. We quickly learned not to walk on those streets as it was the opposite of calm, and we were not interested in those wares. I did not see the snake, but I felt its luring presence. Was there something wrong with me that I no longer wanted those things?

The ferry boats went to a few different islands. We perused the brochures, and determined that we would take a day trip to one of the fanciest islands, St. Matthew, the next day. It was a French island as well, and was famous for attracting celebrities and the wealthiest individuals to visit and to own homes there. It was known for its white-sand beaches, designer shops, high-end restaurants and its yacht-filled harbor. We were curious to see if the super rich had a better life. Why we were still asking that question at the age of seventy is perhaps notable. We remained on a quest to determine what inspired happiness. Undoubtedly we will die not being able to answer that question completely. Despite the fact that we were literally addicted to reading and listening to the news while in New York, we did not do so while on the islands as we determined that we wanted to live in our bubble for a few more days. Even television was on the "no fly" list.

When we arrived in St. Matthew, we rented a car for the day. That island did have the appearance that nobody but the richest lived there. We drove around, and the scenery was quite spectacular. The sky, water, and beaches all deserved the highest marks for natural beauty. From what we could observe, many of the houses were beautifully appointed, inside and out. The landscaping was lush and opulent. The restaurants were filled with patrons with expensive clothes, jewelry and cars. There was a sense of security and stability there which only many generations of money can buy, or a quick influx of extraordinary amounts of cash.

However, the roads were extremely narrow and hilly, and the traffic was alarmingly intense. We pictured a few individuals having too much to drink in the bars downtown, and later careening into other drivers on their way home. We saw a number of car wrecks by the side of the road. This island was also built up to an extreme. The houses were close together and dotted every inch of the hillsides. Rather than feeling serene, we felt that man had impeded upon the perfection of the landscape.

Nonetheless, it satisfied our urge to glimpse into the windows of the homes of the one percent. We did not learn anything new. It seemed as though the shops on Madison Avenue in New York City had been unloaded onto the island paradise. We were not envious. We did not covet what people had. But it did stand in stark contrast to the struggle for survival we observed on the island of St. Francis.

We returned to St. Francis by ferry boat just as it was getting dark. When we disembarked, nobody warned us that there was any problem there. We immediately smelled smoke and wondered where the odor was coming from. We picked up our rental car from the parking lot, and prepared to drive ten minutes to the Dutch side where our rental apartment was located. My husband drove, and I was in the passenger seat. As we started to cruise down the streets in the downtown area, we noticed that there were a lot of tourists sitting outside at restaurants, enjoying drinks and food without a care in the world. There were the sounds of competing music from the different venues, laughter and talking. Even though we were hungry, we decided we would eat once we arrived at the Dutch part of the island. Other than the smell of smoke, there was no sense that anything was amiss.

A few streets away, we came upon a street where there were trash cans on fire, and a dozen shirtless, angry, mostly young, and a few older local men yelling at us. They came up to the windows of our car and surrounded us. Some of them had masks on, others were waving sticks, and a few were holding bottles of alcohol and drinking heavily from the bottles. They told us, in French, that we could not pass there. They had erected a barricade with debris. They did not tell us why.

We quickly turned around and a few streets over came upon a police barricade. There were many police, wearing riot gear, and heavily armed. It reminded us of the security in Grand Central Station in New York City post 9/11, and the police opposition to the yellow jacket demonstrations in France. They told us that we could not pass there. We asked them how we could get to the Dutch side. They shrugged their shoulders, and pointed in the direction of another town.

We asked them what the problem was. They said that there were demonstrations on the French side because of the economic situation after the hurricane. We did not know what they meant, and they were in no position to explain further. They told us to be careful as some demonstrators were using Molotov cocktails, also known as gasoline bombs or a poor man's grenade, which are bottles filled with flammable liquid and a means to ignite them. We observed police officers pointing their weapons into the crowd of angry rioters.

We continued on, with an ever rising sense of terror. We came upon another barricade. Again, there were angry men wielding sticks, drinking alcohol from bottles, and surrounding our car and other cars. There were women and children on the side of the roads. Everybody was outside their homes to see what the demonstrators were going to do. Loud music was blaring.

There was a party atmosphere "gone wrong" that seemed straight out of my vision of hell. They were asking the tourists in their cars for money in order to pass. We gave them some money, and explained that we wanted to make it over to the Dutch side. My husband told them that he was a doctor, and needed to get to the hospital. They seemed to treat us with more respect because of that. He shook as many hands as he could from the car window to appeal to their humanity.

Then we came upon another barricade. But this time we observed completely burned out cars on the side of the road. The "party" was becoming more dangerous. All it would take was one action by one person, and there would be uncontained violence. It seemed that there was no way out. Some tourists were still walking to the restaurants in the midst of these demonstrations, clearly unaware of all that was going on, or not caring. We decided to stop at a hotel we observed in the town. We thought that perhaps if we stayed overnight, everything would die down by the next day and we could safely make it home. Clearly it was not prudent to be on the roads, and we could not find safe passage in any direction.

The French manager at the hotel said there was no room for us. We offered to sleep in the hallway, or anywhere they wanted to put us in the hotel for that night as we feared for our lives. He was indifferent to our plight. He said that he was not responsible for us in any way. One of the workers, named Jude, a father of five children, who later told us that he was Haitian, independently offered to telephone a woman who rented rooms down the road. He called her and obtained a room for us. He then offered to drive our rental car past the demonstrators to those rooms, with us as passengers, which we gratefully accepted. He was warm, concerned, and humane, unlike his boss.

We were told that there was a key in a flower pot by the front door, and we could let ourselves into an area with a few small rooms. Jude waited until he saw us get inside. The complex was empty, there was no kitchen, and no food or drink to be found. Our room was basic, but had a toilet, sink, and bed, which were welcome sights. After we went into our rented room, we realized that we were hungry. I was too scared to leave to walk on the streets to the restaurant. I did not want him to, but my husband ventured out and discovered that everything had closed by then. Upon his return to the room, he reported that there was no food to be found, the rioters controlled the streets, and the other tourists had departed the area. I had one apple and one chocolate bar, which I offered to him as he had medical problems and could not be without food. I was pleased to learn that in these circumstances, I was able to think of another rather than myself. The irony of my offering him an apple in the "Garden of Eden" was not lost on me. In this case, the apple was his temporary salvation rather than his downfall.

My husband had several serious medical conditions, including heart disease and high blood pressure, and needed his medication to control it. He did not bring his medication with him for the next day, as we thought that we were returning to our apartment. Of all things, that was our most serious concern. We turned on the local television and learned that the demonstrators were looting pharmacies, and I imagined a world where we could not get his medication, and there would not be any available to replace it.

In addition, I was afraid that all of the stress was going to give him a heart attack, and that they would not let us pass to go to the hospital. Even if we could get to the hospital, maybe it would be too late. Although not as serious, but humiliating, I was afraid at our age, with our constant use of toilets, we would be in an area without them if we left the room. I tried to shut these thoughts out of my mind, and worked toward an escape solution.

Although we went to sleep for several hours, as we badly needed rest, around 2:00 a.m., we woke up in a panic. We tried to call the embassy, but there was none in the area. We then called the local police. They told us to leave immediately as things were quiet, and that if we tried to leave in the morning, we would not be able to pass the barricades. They had no idea how long the demonstrations would last as these demonstrations came as a complete surprise, were not planned much in advance by the demonstrators, and had erupted spontaneously throughout the French side of the island. They told us that there were four areas where the activity was the most serious, and we were in one of them.

There was little to no coverage of what was happening on this small island on the internet. The television kept repeating old footage. I asked the police officer on the telephone what the demonstrations were about. He explained that from the rioter's perspective, after the hurricane, many locals who had lived in certain areas for generations had lost their homes. They did not technically own the land. Developers were coming in and taking the land away from them. The government was refusing to help the locals to rebuild their homes, and, simultaneously, were delaying the developers. In addition, since the hurricane damage, there was a problem with the water, and the local people were enraged that the government had not rectified the situation for two years.

We empathized with their plight, while not relishing being in the middle of their conflict, and not necessarily approving of their methods of violence and intimidation. We could feel their anger and frustration with all of our senses. We also knew, physically and intellectually, that we had to escape, and quickly. Our circumstances had become Darwinian. We pushed to be out of the way of danger.

We quickly dressed and went to our car. Thankfully, although it was parked on the street in front of the rooms we were staying in, nobody had damaged it and we could drive away. We realized how lucky we were when we saw burned out cars nearby that had not been there several hours earlier. Under optimal circumstances, we were about thirty minutes away from our apartment. As we headed out, the streets were completely empty. There were no rioters, no police, and no moving vehicles. There was garbage and refuse everywhere on the streets and sidewalks. It looked like the aftermath of a parade in hell where nobody had come to clean up the debris. There were barricades still remaining all along the way. In some instances my husband had to drive on the sidewalks to get around them. When we tried to get past one of the barriers, I thought our car was going to turn over. We passed about thirty burned out cars, which looked like upside down skeletons on the side of the road. Some were piled up in the shape of a bonfire and blocked the streets. Our hearts were racing, but we were determined to make it home without incident, and we truly felt that nothing and no one could stop us.

About fifteen minutes into the ride, on a lonely, desolate street, two young men, who seemed more innocent than the other rioters we had encountered, rode up beside our car on motorbikes. They told us that we were not allowed to be there. My husband used all of his charm, and all of the French he knew, to explain that we were headed to the hospital on the Dutch side as he was a doctor. They then offered to show us the way past the barricade, and let us go through. While they had been given the job of guarding the area, they seemed to be on an innocent joy ride. They appeared, also, to be relishing the ego boost of being in charge and ordering us around, which was the sinister counterpoint.

When we finally made it over the border to the Dutch side, we allowed ourselves to breathe again. There was no sense of accomplishment. There was only a feeling of complete exhaustion. What should have been a thirty minute ride took over one hour, but, of course, that was the least of it. We passed no moving vehicles at all on either the French or Dutch side except for the boys on motorbikes.

After we arrived at the apartment, my husband said we needed to get a flight home immediately. We did not know if the situation would worsen, and since we were on the Dutch side, our opportunity was at that moment. We called the airlines. They wanted to charge us extra for changing the flight despite the fact that they had many seats available. We told them we were fleeing a war zone, and they finally relented and agreed to charge us the same amount. We left that day, four hours later. We happily forfeited the rent for the remaining days of our trip. The people from the island who were employed at the rental car agency and at the airport in St. Francis expressed concern to us about the demonstrations. They hoped that they would not lose tourism because of it, and implored us to return to their paradise. We felt a deep sadness over the entire situation.

When we arrived home, we greeted cold and windy New York with tears of gratitude.

Now we felt as though we were in paradise despite the constant threats in the news that something terrible will happen in Manhattan post 9/11. We had heat in our apartment, food in the refrigerator, healthy water, a comfortable bed, a warm shower and a working toilet, and all of Manhattan as our living room. We scoured the news to find out what was going on in St.

Francis after we left. The only news was from their local paper, which said that the rioting and demonstrations went on for five more days. Many businesses were looted and destroyed.

We read that the French army tried to land their boats on the Dutch side to help the police on the French side, but the Dutch would not let them in. We also learned that the reason that the French side was not being repaired as quickly as the Dutch side after the hurricane was because of their bureaucracy. We read confirmatory information that the French part of the island was faced with a situation where the local people were left without adequate housing and the economy was not thriving because tourism was down. The developers could not start developing quickly or repairing to attract more tourism, and to employ more islanders, because of the government, and the problem with the water, a basic need, was not being fixed by the authorities. The wealthy people, of course, could use bottled water and expensive filters.

The day after we came back to New York, we watched the 1981 movie "Escape from New York," starring Kurt Russell. The scenes with Russell navigating the streets littered with barricades, debris, and bombed-out cars reminded us exactly of what we had experienced on St. Francis. Paradise, or hell, or a combination of the two could be anywhere, in our imaginations, on film, or in real life.

I was not certain if watching that movie was helpful for post traumatic stress. There have been other times since our island riot experience where I have experienced those same feelings of rising adrenaline and the need to escape. Demonstrations, parades, crowds of angry people, crowded elevators, are all ripe for bringing those feelings to the fore. Although I continue to travel to experience other cultures, I no longer anticipate paradise wherever I go. I expect that we will have to navigate whatever problems we encounter wherever we are. I always have comfortable shoes on, and a bag with zippered compartments, with all of my essentials, including my passport, which fits neatly under my coat. I insist that my husband take his medication with him, even on day trips. We have wisdom from biting the apple. You never know where you will encounter the snake, and you never know if you will find kindness and humanity.

Chapter Three

When Did You Know It Was Over

*"In the long run, we shape our lives, and we shape ourselves.
The process never ends until we die. And the choices we make are
ultimately our own responsibility."*

—Eleanor Roosevelt

There were six of us who met at an Ivy League school in the 1970's. All of our first marriages eventually ended in divorce. That was the strongest tie that bound us, and compelled us to meet for a long weekend once a year at a house on Cape Cod, which belonged to one of the group. We looked forward to seeing one another, but simultaneously dreaded it on some level because we usually touched upon difficult topics during our many free-ranging discussions.

While there was a lot of mutual support, there was a subtle competition amongst us too. Sometimes it was about who would win the "award" for most professionally successful, and other times it was for who had the most negative things happen to them. Consistently it was about who was aging the best from a beauty point of view, as well as physically and mentally. All of us read Mary McCarthy's "The Group," but we were aware that she discussed a different time and place as a backdrop for her women. We considered ourselves more evolved.

One year, when we were in our sixties, at our self-made annual reunion, we decided to talk about when we each knew that our first marriages were over. Most of us were panicked about the fact that all kinds of our relationships had ended over time. Some were breaks with family, others were professional divorces, and there were instances of long and short term friendships lost. As we aged, these losses were becoming more painful rather than easier. We thought that if we dissected what happened to our first marriages, it might give us insight into other relationships and how best to handle letting go. Since it was my idea to talk about this topic, I began the discussion. The group called me Cissie, although my real name was Cecily. I will give you some background first.

Daniel was my first husband. I met him at college during sophomore year, and we married after graduation. He was a "golden" boy in every way. He had blonde hair, an athletic build, handsome features, and a sharp mind. He enjoyed a good time, but was also disciplined. He was on track to inherit the successful family business. I considered myself sublimely lucky to have found him and to have fallen in love with him, and he with me. I pictured a stable life with a loving husband and father, and a good provider.

All members of the group attended my wedding. We had the ceremony in Maine outside of his parents' summer home. His family owned a chain of pharmacies. He attended a Doctor of Pharmacy graduate school at the University of Michigan, and I earned a Masters of Fine Arts there. After graduation, we moved to the East Coast, and he became employed in the family business helping to run the pharmacies.

We had two healthy children, a comfortable home, and I had the added benefit of a studio in the attic for my painting. Eventually I taught art at a local community center. Our lives were busy and fulfilling. Everything started falling apart when Daniel was in his forties. I told the group:

"You all know the overarching reason why I left Daniel. You all know why it took me a long time to leave him. He was a warm and generous man. He worked hard and he cared. He was adventuresome and funny. But when he started to take prescription drugs to take the edge off the pressure of his work life and family responsibilities, it all started to fall apart. His father had an alcohol problem, so addiction was not new to his family line.

I brought Daniel to rehab multiple times. He always promised he had his habit under control. I went to therapy with him. I learned later that he was lying to both me and the therapist about the extent of his drug habit. I knew things had taken a turn for the worse when he lost a lot of weight and could not sleep through the night. I heard from his coworkers that he was disappearing for ever-increasing periods of time during the work day. He said that rehab did not help him, and he did not want to return.

His personality started to change more dramatically. He lost all of the light, gentle and fun parts of his personality. He became enraged at the slightest provocation. One of our daughters spilled milk in the kitchen, and he went into a tirade. Our son did not want to do his homework, and he banished him to his room for an entire day without meals. I became increasingly fearful for the children. I thought Daniel was setting a terrible example, and, as time went on, I was worried that he would harm the children inadvertently.

Was there a single moment when I knew that our relationship was over? Perhaps that is too simplistic. For me it was an ever building and mounting anxiety about what his unstable personality, as a result of his drug addiction, would do next. If there was one moment in time, it was when we were sitting around the dinner table as a family in the dining room. The children were talking about what they had learned in school. Our daughter asked permission to attend a social at her school, and a sleepover afterwards at her best friend's house. My husband was against it. Our daughter started to argue with him and told him that he was not being a good father. He took a porcelain dish containing pasta, and threw it at the window behind him. It shattered the glass window, and the spaghetti flew around the room.

It was at that moment that I knew that I had to end things with him to protect myself and the children. I had tried everything to help to heal him, and I knew that I did not have the strength to keep fighting for him. The next day I contacted a divorce attorney, and planned my exit.

Do I ever regret that decision? No. Daniel died of an overdose a few years after the divorce, as you know. While it was tragic, it was inevitable, and I was glad that our children were somewhat removed from his orbit when it happened. My first job was to protect them. Will I mourn our relationship and his death for the rest of my life? Absolutely. My only regret is that I could not save him from himself. I knew our marriage was over when I became convinced that he would never control his addiction. His father died of cirrhosis of the liver even though he promised his wife he would stop drinking, which he never did. There were no surprise endings here."

Robin, another member of our group, was a young mother when her marriage ended in divorce. She met her husband in graduate school. They both studied business and each went into lucrative jobs in the financial sector. While on paper they were compatible, in that they both came from similar upper middle class families, there was no real chemistry between them. They both settled, and that was satisfactory for a time. They bought a house, feathered the nest, went out to expensive restaurants, and took luxurious vacations.

A few years into the marriage, they decided to have a child. Once she gave birth to her daughter, Robin determined that she would stay home with her until she was school age. Her husband supported her in that decision as his salary was ample enough to provide for the family. They both had stay-at-home mothers when they were growing up, and for them, it seemed the right thing to do. None of their friends had children yet, and they stopped seeing them because their lives had become so different. Robin did not feel that she had time to make new friends as she was so wrapped up in being a first-time mother.

During the first year of their child's life, Robin became depressed as some new mothers do. Once she was no longer earning a paycheck, her husband became increasingly assertive about how the money he earned should be spent. He criticized her purchases, and wanted to decide everything, down to the cost allocated for the diapers. She resented her loss of status, power and control. They fought bitterly over money. He gave her an allowance, which demoralized her. She thought about returning to work, but she was committed to being home with the baby. She wanted to make the "sacrifice," and was critical of other mothers who were not willing to do the same.

She, in turn, had professionalized her mother status. She breastfed, and did not like the way he gave their child the bottle from her expressed milk. She told him that the way he held the bottle was causing the child distress, and that he did not burp her enough. He did not relish being told what to do, and felt that it emasculated him. He no longer wanted to help with that, and stopped doing the one feeding at midnight.

Robin wanted the baby to sleep in their room. Her husband refused and would not let that happen. When the baby woke up in the middle of the night, on occasion, her husband would enter the nursery, pat the baby in the crib, and then let her cry until she fell asleep. He complained that he was not alert enough at work when he had to tend to the baby at night, and that Robin was home all day and could take naps to make up for the loss of sleep. Robin thought babies should be held when they cried, and she ended up doing all of the night work. The baby would cry whenever her husband held her, which made him want to hold her even less, day or night.

Robin criticized the way he diapered the child, so he stopped doing that. Once the baby started eating solid food, she told her husband that he was feeding her too fast. She pureed all of the food, while he was fine with giving the baby food from jars. When they went outside for outings, Robin did not feel that he dressed the child warmly enough, and always added an extra layer. On the weekends, her husband wanted to go out with the baby to places which would be interesting for adults. Robin was exhausted and wanted to stay home more.

For vacation, he wanted to leave the baby with his or her parents. Robin was not comfortable leaving their child for an extended period of time. He wanted date nights and she was concerned about leaving the baby with a babysitter at that age. They never spent time alone with one another. He grew resentful of her attention to the baby.

The battle lines were drawn about each and every decision. Neither was willing to communicate their feelings in a calm, constructive way, and neither was willing to compromise. Her husband started to come home from work later and later. Robin became upset because she needed a break from child care. She felt conflicted about leaving the baby with a babysitter, and there were no family members around to assist. She became ever more isolated.

Their sex life was nonexistent. She was still hurting from the caesarean section, and the trauma to her body. Her hormones and exhaustion made her feel completely asexual. The breast-feeding took away the sexuality of her breasts. She was depressed and anxious which cut down on her libido. For her husband, in turn, he was no longer attracted to her fatter figure, and flabby stomach, although he chided himself for feeling that way. He no longer touched her, nor did he speak words of endearment. She no longer dressed up for him, and wore oversized clothes. She rarely brushed her hair or put on makeup. Her entire life was centered around the baby's needs. She did not have enough energy to consider his needs, and he felt completely rejected. He, in turn, did nothing to make her feel better. Robin told us:

"There was a slow slog to the finish line of our divorce. There was not enough love between us to sustain the difficult first year of parenthood. Our parenting styles were completely different. Our needs were not compatible. We did not cut each other any slack. Was there a defining moment when I knew the marriage was over? Perhaps one incident was the decisive one.

I had asked my husband to babysit our child one Saturday as I had a haircut appointment. I had not had my hair cut in three months. Note that I said babysit, because he was not a co-equal parenting partner. I dressed in real pants with a zipper instead of stretch pants for the first time in months and months, put on some makeup, sprayed on some perfume, and left for my appointment. I felt almost human. I expressed milk into bottles, set everything up for him, and left written instructions.

When I returned home, I opened the front door. I heard the baby wailing. I waited to hear how long my husband would let the baby cry. He was watching a sporting event in front of the television set in our family room, and drinking wine. He did not see that I had come into the house. I had no idea how long he let her cry before I arrived. I waited five more minutes, and he still did not budge. The crying continued and became more desperate.

I went to the nursery to calm the baby, packed my bags, and left that night with our child for my parent's house. I drove two hours to get there. I never returned. I had known for a long time that he did not love me in the way I needed to be loved. He felt the same way about me.

But when it dawned upon me that he would not care for our child the way I felt the child needed to be cared for, I knew that there was nothing left between us. I did not want our child to grow up in a loveless home."

Nadia's background was quite different from the rest of us. Her parents were born in Russia and became United States citizens. Shortly after graduation from graduate school, Nadia married a boy with a Russian background her parents set her up with. He, too, was born in the United States, and was the son of a Russian family in the community she grew up in. Both Nadia and her husband became scientists, and they worked in separate labs. Nadia told us:

"I had a different problem from the one Robin described. I had too much family 'support' from my husband's side. Three months after our first child was born, my husband's parents moved into our house. My husband insisted upon it, and I did not argue. I had some concerns, but was willing to see how it would work out. My parents ran a small business together, and could not take the time to help much.

At first I was grateful because I could go back to work without the concerns about child care so many of my colleagues had. I knew that the baby was well cared for. If the baby had a fever, my in-laws were there to help. I never had to miss work. My mother-in-law made dinner each night, which was ready when we came home from work, and she did the laundry. She even packed lunch for me with homemade foods. My husband's parents and my parents told me that I should have a second child quickly so that I could get the early childhood needs over with in close succession. As a dutiful daughter, I had our second child eighteen months after the first.

When I had the second girl, my in-laws did not hide their disappointment that I did not give birth to a boy. For medical reasons, the doctor told me I could not have a third child. Their disappointment was permanent.

When my friends and colleagues heard about the arrangement I had with my in-laws, they told me that I was the luckiest mother they knew. I kept asking myself why I did not feel that way and would have preferred a babysitter we paid for. My father-in-law was a quiet man. He did not help much, but he did not get in the way. He mostly read and met his friends at the local diner. I probably could have lived with him forever because he was so low maintenance.

My problem was with my mother-in-law. She never thought that I was good enough for her son, and made it clear that I was fortunate, and perhaps undeserving, to have him as my husband. She took complete control over my household. She ran our kitchen. She ran how things were done for the baby. She ordered me around as if it was her home and not mine. She criticized me for not doing enough for her son. She emphasized how he needed free time, and that since I was the mother, I did not, even though my husband and I had similar jobs.

She talked loudly on the telephone to her friends and told them how lazy I was, and how much the household depended on her doing everything. She told them how I did not seem to understand children and what they needed. She said all of these things to me directly, to my husband, and in front of the children. I wondered what the children would think of me after listening to her, once they understood.

My husband was completely under his mother's spell. He told me that nobody could cook like his mother. He recounted all the favorite foods she made for him when he was younger, and continued to make for him. He complimented her on her excellent housekeeping skills, and the way in which she interacted with and provided for the children. He did not credit my work in the laboratory as a scientist, and he held a dim view of my abilities as a parent and wife. Our time as a couple had been completely destroyed by the presence of my in-laws. We had no privacy.

Was there a moment when I knew the marriage was over? Every moment that my mother-in-law lived under our roof was a moment leading to that eventuality. There was one occurrence which confirmed what I already knew. Her cruelty knew no bounds, nor did her narcissism. I was diagnosed with breast cancer and had to undergo radiation and chemotherapy. I continued to work throughout the treatments, and purchased a good wig after I lost my hair.

One day my mother-in-law told me that my children would never be able to depend on me, and would need her, because I could die at any time. My diagnosis had never been that my cancer was terminal, and she knew that. I told my husband that either he would tell his parents to leave our home, or I would leave with the children. He would not tell his parents to leave.

When my parents heard what happened, they offered to have me and the children live with them. I took them up on it, and went through a terrible court battle for custody. I eventually won, and I have been cancer free. My husband is still living with his mother. My father-in-law died soon after the trial began. He was heartbroken about the fighting, and did not have the strength for it or the aftermath. My children visit with my ex-husband and his mother on a schedule. It is stressful for all of us, but far more free for me. The escape was not easy, but it was worth it. I can clean, do our own laundry, pack our own lunches, and make our dinner. I earn enough that I can hire help for some of it if I choose to. I was a capable and loving mother, and no one could take that away from me."

Debbie had her own issues around motherhood. Debbie met her husband in law school. They both became corporate lawyers at large firms. They had long hours, continual pressure, and a high-end lifestyle. They eventually purchased a penthouse apartment, and hired a famous decorator to create an atmosphere of luxury they wanted to convey. When they met, and before they married, they discussed the fact that neither one of them wanted children. They preferred to dote on one another, to have free time after work to spend as they pleased, and to travel the world.

The reason Debbie did not want children had to do with her family of origin. She grew up as the eldest in a family of five children. She was responsible for a lot of the up-bringing of her siblings, and felt that she had lost much of her childhood doing so. She no longer wanted those responsibilities. Her siblings still depended on her emotionally, and she frequently had to help them out with her time and money.

Her husband was a child of divorce. In his view, he never received enough attention from his own parents, so he relished the attention Debbie gave to him. She took care of his errands, and all household matters. She purchased his clothes, arranged for his dry cleaning, made his doctor appointments, took care of their meals, and made all social arrangements. She hired people for whatever needed to be done in their apartment. She planned their vacations, and made all of the reservations. She was happy to do everything for him, and he felt loved being taken care of in that way. Taking care of one person was easier for her than all she had to do for her family in the past. Debbie told us:

"We went along for many years in our happy bubble. We were fulfilling each other's needs. I was a giver, and he was a taker. Then, things started to change. My husband was in his early forties. He went through some kind of crisis, and decided that he wanted to have a child, and would not be happy without one. I was about the same age. My gynecologist told me that I had gone into early menopause and would not be able to have a child. One night, I told my husband this news over dinner. He looked more despondent than I had ever seen him.

We talked about whether we could adopt. I told him that I would consider that option if it meant so much to him. He said that he was not interested in adopting. He wanted his own genes passed down, which, for him, was the whole point of why he wanted a child. He wanted to leave a legacy. We were both reluctant to think about getting eggs from a donor, or renting a womb. For him, the uncertainty of the genetic material of the eggs made it an unacceptable option for him.

For the first time in our relationship, I did not know how to provide for him. He became more depressed. He spent more time at work. He started to drink more wine at dinner. Instead of the usual glass, he began to drink the entire bottle. He started to spend more time on his computer, and began to come to bed after he knew I was asleep. The closeness we had shared began to dissolve with this one irreconcilable problem.

How did I know the marriage was over? One late night, I heard noises which indicated that my husband was still awake. He had not been to bed as his side was unruffled. I listened when he went into the bathroom. I walked into the room where his computer was open. He was chatting with a woman online. I saw that he was talking about wanting a child, and so was she. It was clear from their discussion that this was not their first online encounter. When he came out of the bathroom, he looked startled when he saw me, and then his face looked guilty when he saw that I had read his screen.

My husband admitted to me that he wanted to find the right kind of woman to marry, with intelligence and grace, who could bear his child. He cried, and told me that he thought about it night and day, and did not want to die without a child of his own. I realized at that moment that there was nothing that could save our marriage. I asked him to move out the next morning. He understood."

Lisa, another member of our group, ended up in a long distance relationship with her first husband. They were both doctors who met in medical school. For many years, they lived and worked in the same city, and raised their children. Several years ago, in their late fifties, he was given the opportunity to chair a department in a different city approximately two thousand seven hundred miles away. She had her commitments in her private practice, and could not move without giving up her career. Their children were adults and living on their own.

They talked about it endlessly, and agreed that he should take the job and they would make their long distance relationship work. Lisa and her then husband tried to work out conditions which would ensure that their relationship would last. They would facetime each day before bed. They would email at least once during the day. They would spend one weekend out of each month together. They would alternate who would have to travel. They would spend all their vacations together. They would try to attend some professional conferences together depending on work schedules. For two years they were able to make the situation work. They tried not to be jealous when one mentioned that they had lunch or dinner with an opposite sex colleague. Lisa said:

"In many of our stories in this group, there was an unraveling of our relationships despite best intentions. During the year that things started to go downhill, I fell on an icy sidewalk and broke my leg in many places. It required surgery, which then had some complications.

Simultaneously, my husband's work had become more demanding. I could not travel to him, and his work demands were keeping him from coming home as often as we had agreed to. He stayed with me only one day after my surgery, and then returned to his other home. That was disappointing to me. He told me that his work was the reason, but I will never really know. I felt vulnerable and abandoned. At the time I did not know if my feelings of vulnerability stemmed from my injury or from what I perceived as his lack of attention and care. I thought that perhaps he was having an affair. I recounted in my head all of the times that he put his career before me. Perhaps he was counting the times I did the same to him.

I told my husband that I was tired of our long distance relationship, and begged him to obtain employment close to home. I reasoned that as we age, we would need to take care of each other more and more. He was satisfied with his work career, and did not think that he could duplicate the job he had closer to home. I asked him whether he would be willing to take a job with less responsibility to be nearer to me. He said no. He asked me if I would be willing to start a new practice where he was and give my practice up where I had been for over three decades. I told him that was impossible at my age. He asked me if I were willing to take a job with less responsibility to be near to him. I replied no.

My orthopedist was a divorced man in his late sixties. He treated me throughout my issues with my leg. He was close to retirement, and seemed to take an inordinate interest in me. He asked me to come for more appointments than I thought necessary. He asked me to dinner.

I was lonely, he was lonely and so I went. And there it began. I felt guilty about the affair, but I did not want to be alone. After three months I told my husband that I met someone else and that we would need to get divorced. He was relieved. He had met someone else too, a colleague, months before. I guess we were 'good catches' to have so easily replaced one another. Or perhaps we both knew that there was no solution to our intractable problem. We were each 'married' to our careers in the sense that our work came before our marriage. It was not as simple as all that, but in the end, it was the best solution for both of us. We did our best, but our best was not good enough to sustain our relationship, despite having raised children together."

Valerie was the last member of our tight-knit group to speak her truth. She was also the last member of our group to get married the first time. Valerie never had much of an interest in the idea of getting married while we were in college. She was an art history major who became a curator. She was a free spirit. She was not a planner. When she turned thirty-five, she started to panic. All of her friends had married at least once and most of her friends had children already. What if she wanted children? Her mother told her that she better settle down, or she would lose her chance.

She decided that she could no longer wait for love. She had to make a marriage of convenience, and she was determined to find someone tolerable. She met her husband on a dating website. He was nice looking in a conservative, lacoste shirt, khaki pants way. He was not her usual type, which was a moody artist with long hair, wearing jeans and a sweatshirt. But her type had not worked for her in terms of starting a family.

Her husband-to-be owned parking garages in different parts of the country. It was lucrative, and he did not have to work much. His employees managed most of the work. He was interested in art, so he would attend gallery openings, academic lectures and museum events with her. One night he surprised her with tickets to Las Vegas, and he arranged for Elvis to marry them. It was not her style, but it was funky enough to be amusing. She went along with it.

After that, she moved into his place as he had a big loft space, and she had a tiny apartment. Not much unusual happened until she answered their telephone at their loft one evening. Valerie told us that she heard startling news which was the precipitating event for her divorce:

"My husband said that he needed to travel on business to another state where he had parking garages. I was home alone. The telephone rang. We had a landline. A woman's voice asked me if I was Valerie. I told her yes. She said that she had unusual information for me. My curiosity was aroused. She said that my husband was married to her, she had two children with him, and they never divorced. Her husband (my husband) was with her now, but had gone to work. He accidentally left his cell phone at home, she tried the password of his date of birth, and was able to get in. She found emails, texts and telephone calls to me, and was able to piece it together. She did not know that I had married her husband too, thinking it was just an affair.

I considered myself an intellectual, artistic and spiritual person. Simultaneously, I was street smart. No one would describe me as gullible. I pictured this situation being aired on some bad television talk show about people who were nothing like me. But there I was with a woman sobbing on the other end of the line, with sounds of her children, my husband's children, in the background.

Our conversation continued. She texted me photographs of her wedding with him, and their marriage certificate. He used the same name for that certificate, with slightly different spelling. He had told me that both of his parents were dead, and that he had no siblings. She texted me photographs of his parents and siblings at their wedding. My husband looked just like his father, and one of his brothers. She provided me with enough evidence that I was certain that she had married my husband. She texted me a selfie of her with him, which she took that day before he left their home, wearing the same clothes he was wearing when he left me at our apartment.

I told her not to tell him anything right away. She agreed. I needed time to move and to make arrangements with lawyers. He was not due back for another week, which would give me enough time to begin to extricate him from my life. When he contacted me before he came home, I pretended that nothing had happened.

By the time he returned, I had moved all of my things out of his loft. I did not leave a note. I did not tell him where I had moved to. I never spoke with him again. I let my lawyer handle everything. My lawyer told him to never contact me again, which he did not. I spoke with his wife and kept her apprised of my situation. I did not know how she was going to handle things on her end, given that she had small children with him. I felt more sorry for her than I did for myself.

My story had a surprise ending. My lawyer was a single man in his early forties. He had decided a few years earlier that he was ready to get married and start a family, but he had not met the right person yet. We were attracted to one another, and he helped me out of a situation when I was at my lowest. You all know him as my current husband, but perhaps you did not know how it all began. My therapist told me not to jump into a relationship too soon with him since I was vulnerable. I did not listen to her, even though she was right, but my instincts that time worked out. I am a trusting soul. Things do not always go well for those like me, but in that circumstance it did."

Our annual weekend ended with all of us feeling closer to one another for having shared intimate memories, failures and successes. We vowed that we would continue to meet each year, and that perhaps if we out-lived our husbands and lovers, we would move into a big house together, and take care of one another for our remaining years. The idea did not seem outrageous. That would be a not so surprise ending.

Chapter Four

Is Being Rude More Serious Than Just Being Crude?

"Emotions are contagious. We've all known it experientially. You know after you have a really fun coffee with a friend, you feel good. When you have a rude clerk in a store, you walk away feeling bad."

—Daniel Goleman

"A rude nature is worse than a brute nature by so much more as man is better than a beast: and those that are of civil natures and genteel dispositions are as much nearer to celestial creatures as those that are rude and cruel are to devils."

—Margaret Cavendish

Once or twice a year I had the opportunity to spend time with my closest friend from law school days, Helene. She lived on the East Coast and I lived on the West Coast, but we made it our business to maintain our life-long friendship. Each visit, in what had become a ritual, we met at our favorite family-owned diner in Manhattan where we sat for hours discussing personal and political issues, interchangeably. The staff never rushed us to leave, we had our coffee cups refilled continually without asking, and we shared a muffin big enough to feed a family. Most importantly we fed each other's souls. We always left a big tip. Everybody was happy.

In 2020, when we were in our late sixties, we arranged to meet at the same diner after Helene was finished with work. She was a partner in a medium-sized firm, specializing in commercial litigation. She came from a wealthy family and her husband earned a high salary as the CEO of a small company. Money was never a problem for her. She had children and grandchildren. I was on vacation from my work as an immigration attorney, fighting difficult battles each day on behalf of immigrant families. My husband had died when my children were young, and I earned a relatively low salary for my work, although I was deeply committed to it. Money was always a problem for me. I too had grandchildren. Our lives had always been busy and complicated.

Helene arrived in a state of agitation. She had undergone knee replacement surgery, and was walking with a cane. After she sat down and arranged herself comfortably in the booth, she said that she had a difficult journey in order to meet me. Helene said that after she left her office, a bicyclist, riding on the sidewalk, nearly ran into her. He did not apologize. A few blocks later, a woman with an oversized handbag pushed past her and practically knocked her over. The woman looked at Helene disdainfully, as if Helene's walking slowly was a deliberate attempt to thwart her from getting where she needed to go quickly.

When Helene managed to hobble down the subway stairs to the track, she was elated because the train arrived quickly.

When she entered the subway car, nobody offered her a seat despite the fact that she was standing for over five stops holding her cane, in obvious discomfort. Then, before she met me, she went into a drugstore to purchase some medication for her headache. The woman in front of her as she entered the store did not hold the door open for her. A man jumped the line ahead of her as she waited to pay for the medicine. The employee behind the counter barely looked at Helene when she made the purchase.

Helene said that in general she was able to cope with these rudenesses, which unfortunately had become a fact of modern life, but this particular day had been fraught with incivility, which had made her more vulnerable to slights. She said that before work, instead of doing meditation, she made the unfortunate choice of watching the news. In displays of divisive partisan politics, she heard our top political leaders engaging in name calling, inappropriate showings of anger, and a refusal to value each other's ideas. These were not mere heated conversations. Perhaps political figures were influencing how we all treated one another. It was "trickle down" rudeness. Does self-interest trump everything these days? If we bully, humiliate, demand, yell, name call and refuse to listen, do we "get our way?" Do we "win"?

Then, she put in her earpods, and listened to the radio on the way to work. More vicious attacks, name calling, and slights from many different quarters. On the subway, she watched a TV reality show on her ipad. More insults and demeaning behaviors. She felt under siege. She vowed to read a book of her choosing on her ipad next time. To some extent, she had voluntarily submitted to the culture the media was serving.

She mentioned that once she arrived at work, along with her morning coffee, opposing counsel on a case cursed at her over the telephone and called her a bitch. We both recalled how in 1977, more than two decades ago, the then Chief Justice of the New York Court of Appeals had promulgated a civility code for "combative attorneys and supercilious judges." This was not a new issue.

Later in the day, Helene recalled, a young associate in the firm came into her office, closed the door, and started to cry. She told Helene that a powerful partner in the firm had called her an aggressive, fat Jew because they had disagreed about how to handle a particular matter.

Helene was still processing that event and how to handle it. These were examples of when people did not care that they offended others. There was an obvious absence of decency evident in these events.

As lawyers and concerned citizens, we agreed that incivility, rudeness, lack of respect, and a climate of fear, suspicion, apathy, anger, vengefulness and hopelessness leads to threatening behaviors and even crimes. What we were talking about was more than politeness and good manners. It was about acknowledging the value of other people. It was about respect for laws, rules and norms to guide all of us as to what is acceptable and unacceptable behavior. Rules of civility are rules of morality, we told each other. Manners are entangled with ethics. We recalled our mandatory class on ethics in law school. Although we worshiped different religions, we had learned ethical values in our houses of worship, and in our homes. We recognized that there is a connection between civility and being a good citizen and a good person.

We knew that people, during all ages, were sometimes disrespectful, vindictive, cruel and judgmental. Had rudeness gotten worse, we asked ourselves? How would our children and grandchildren fare in all of this? We had taught them to be compassionate. We emphasized that we are all equal members of the human race. We taught them the golden rule to "do unto others as you would have them do unto you." We told them that if you treat others with respect, you create a positive environment such that it is more likely that others will treat you that way. Were we doing enough? Helene even gave her children a book about manners by Emily Post.

After we had this conversation, we decided to informally poll some of our friends to learn about their experiences with rudeness. Perhaps even with our decades of having been toughened up as litigators, we were too sensitive, and too easily bruised? We agreed that we would get back together in six months to compare notes, which we did, at the same diner. The incidents described to us occurred in every environment including at work, at school, in stores, as part of the political fray, and on social media. Stories abound anywhere where humans can be found.

Here is a small sampling of what we learned.

One friend mentioned that he was a successful leader in his organization for more than twenty years. One day he was called into the office of his superiors in the administration. They told him that he would have to leave in four weeks although he had not received any bad reviews or complaints. He was given no notice about his performance, and virtually no opportunity to be heard. They eventually hired a younger person to replace him. He was lucky to land on his feet at an even better job with more responsibility, so by all accounts he bettered his situation.

Nonetheless, after all he had given to his original job, the lack of respect he was shown had been a hurt he cannot shake. It haunted him, and he lost some trust. He became even more vigilant that he would bring the power of kindness to every encounter he had, in all contexts.

Another individual said he was regularly teased at work by his co-workers about his weight and height. He was a genial, good-natured fellow, and pretended he did not care. Every time there was a birthday cake for someone at the office, he was mocked. One time, when he was humiliated about his short stature, he told his co-worker that where he comes from, the measure of a man is from the neck up. He eventually left that job because he was tired of pretending that the slights and humiliations did not matter. He did not fit into the culture, nor did he want to.

Another friend, who is a world-renowned professor with many publications and awards to his credit, recalled his college days. He went to an exclusive, snobby, all-male college where most of the students were Protestants from wealthy families and had boarding school backgrounds. He was from a working-class Irish background, went to Catholic schools, and was admitted to the college on scholarship. There were very few scholarships given at that time. He said that he was reminded of the socio-economic, class and religious differences between him and the others almost every day, and was shunned by some of the students and faculty. One professor even called him a "mick," and implied that he must be drunk, like "so many of his brethren" when he gave a response to a question posed by the professor which the professor did not like. He spent the rest of his career proving his professor, and the other bullies, wrong.

One woman of Mexican descent told me that she went for a haircut. She did not have a Mexican last name as she used her husband's when she made the appointment. When she arrived at the hair salon, once they saw her brown skin, she was treated rudely by staff. She was kept waiting longer than anyone else. Women who arrived after her were taken first. The woman who washed her hair turned the water on so hot she felt she had been scalded, and when the employee combed her hair, she did it so roughly she pulled out chunks. The man who cut her hair botched it badly in that it was completely uneven, so she had to go elsewhere to have it fixed. She observed that he gave perfect haircuts to the other women who were there that day.

She felt demeaned, and went on the internet and gave the salon a scathing review. The salon then offered her a free haircut. She declined.

We had a mutual friend who ran in a primary election against an African-American candidate for political office. The local African-American newspaper published an article in which the writer called our friend a racist. African-American district leaders tried to convince party members that the only reason our friend was running was to ruin the chances of their candidate because of race. Our friend was a member of Ethical Culture, and his parents were part of the civil rights movement. He and his family were deeply committed to equality for all. He was a humanist and a scholar. These lies about his being a racist left scarring, and our friend refused to run for political office again.

One of my friends, who was a Democrat, posted on social media that she could not be friendly with or associate with anyone who supported then President Donald Trump. Likewise, a Republican friend regularly posted scathing cartoons and text messages about Democratic elected officials and candidates. Helene and I shared that we cannot invite many friends with different political persuasions to our homes for a party. The polarization ran deep, and was fueled by great passion on both sides. We had both been on debate teams at college. It was difficult to conceive that issues could not be discussed in a different manner. Nobody seems to know how to move forward with this.

Helene and I started to delve into stories we heard about childhood memories of rudeness and incivility to see where that would take us. These were "mean girls" and "mean boys" stories.

One friend recalled that she was sitting in the schoolyard of the elementary school with her girlfriend, when an older boy who was already in middle school arrived. Both she and her friend were worried about attending middle school the following year, as they had been happy at their elementary school. They expressed those fears to the boy. He told my friend that the people who were popular in elementary school would not necessarily be popular in middle school, and that she was definitely not going to be one of the popular ones. She did not ask for further clarification, and went home to her mother and cried all evening. The possibility of exclusion was a fate nobody wanted at that young age.

Another friend recalled how she was sitting in a pizza shop after school with her girlfriends when they were in high school. They had been discussing her behind her back, and held an "intervention." They told her that they had been talking about how to tell her, but did not know how. They handed her a can of spray underarm deodorant. They even put a bow on it as if it was a present. They urged her to use it, and told her that she needed to wash her hair and face more often, and recommended a dermatologist. She felt a great deal of shame, as there were three of them and one of her. It was hardly a private conversation. After the "intervention," they began to discuss a girl who was popular with the boys. They mentioned all the boys they thought she had sex with, and referred to her as a "slut." My friend had no idea how she felt about sex at that point, as she was inexperienced, but she knew that what they were saying was another form of shaming. She could not recall if she joined that conversation to fit in or not. She hoped she did not.

Several individuals recalled an incident which occurred in their high school. A group of boys had rated about thirty high school girls according to their body parts, and other characteristics, their purported sexual activities, and many other categories. The boys posted their ratings on social media. The parents, when they found out, were outraged, the school became involved, as did the police, and the boys faced charges. Many of the girls were traumatized. Helene and I recalled several such lists being passed around in our day, although there was no social media to post it on. The vast reach of technology made it all so much worse.

One gay friend told me that while in high school, before he "came out," he was repeatedly ridiculed by other students, and even the gym teacher, for the way he dressed, walked and talked. They would mimic him and laugh derisively. He said that it had become so difficult and painful that he decided to graduate early so that he could move and go to college in a town which had more acceptance of all kinds of people. He felt that the harassment he had endured for many years had shaped his world, and that he still had nightmares about it so many years later. He has been in therapy for many years to help him cope.

Helene recalled that she attended an Ivy League university. There was another college in the same town. The young men outnumbered the young women at the Ivy League school. Many of the young men told Helene that they would never date the "dogs," meaning the "ugly women" at the Ivy League school, and that they would only date the "good looking" women at the other college. Helene mentioned that she felt demeaned and angry, at the same time, by these comments, whether they were referring to her specifically or not.

A friend from law school told me about an incident which occurred at the end of their third year. There was a party in the downstairs lobby of the building for the graduating class which was planned by a group of students. There were tables with food and soft drinks set up, and a welcoming collegial atmosphere.

All were proud of having completed a rigorous, intellectual course of study, and were looking forward to their summer jobs and new careers. The professors were mingling with the students.

All of a sudden, a woman dressed in a short skirt, and low cut blouse, walked into the lobby. She read a "strip-o-gram. She turned on her boombox, which played strip tease music, set it down on the floor, and started to writhe and tear off her clothes down to her underwear. Naturally many of the male law students were clapping and cheering. None of the professors commented or tried to stop the woman. Some of the male professors were joining in the "fun." The female law students, for the most part, were troubled, but none wanted to appear as though they were "prudish." Perhaps it was an initiation into the male-dominated legal world they were entering. At that time, when lawyers were waiting in a courtroom for calendars to be called, there were very few women. Perhaps it was a reminder of the beauty queen pageants and porn star world of popular culture. Helene and I did not think we would have been happier if we heard that there was a male stripper there too. We both felt it was a rude, demeaning experience because the audience was not able to voluntarily choose to participate. They were a captive audience at a professional function.

After discussing these incidents and more, Helene and I, who had both traveled extensively, turned our discussion to ethnic differences and how the perception of rudeness changed depending on the culture, both nationally and internationally. Obviously there was good and bad in each country or state. Rudeness has been defined as "a display of disrespect by not complying with the social norms or etiquette of a group or culture. These norms have been established as the essential boundaries of normally accepted behavior." We thought of a few examples from our travels, and shared notes.

Helene mentioned that she went to New Zealand recently, and found that, overall, people were friendlier, more civil and kinder than in other places in the world. Simply put, they smiled more. She did not experience a single incident of rudeness, and she wondered why. She told me that she discussed this with some New Zealanders, and asked them for their theories on why this was so. The sum of what they told her was that there was more physical space for everybody, and therefore less opportunity for someone to put their own needs first. They said that there was less of an obvious distinction between economic classes, more opportunity, and therefore reduced competition, and more overall satisfaction. They said that from an early age, there was an emphasis in the schools on morals, ethics and decency.

We agreed that it was hard to gauge the cultural differences in China because of the language barrier. We both noticed that in some urban areas, people routinely spit on the street, and pushed each other on public transportation and on the street. We noticed the pushing in Israel too, and other places in the Middle East, where if you did not push, you might not get onto the bus or into a particular location at all. Nobody said "excuse me." In Japan, they had separate subway cars for men and women so that there was no inappropriate touching. In England, everyone stood neatly on line and nobody tried to cut in front. At least this was true in our experience.

In France, you had to try to speak French. People seemed ruder in Paris than in other places in France, especially at restaurants. You had to say hello in a polite way before anyone would address you civilly when you entered any establishment. People were smiling less, especially in Paris, with the frequent strikes, and the clash of cultures with the immigrant population trying to integrate itself into a society with strict rules and norms.

I mentioned that I recently spent time in major cities in Florida and in Texas, and that the employees at the airports, hotels, stores, restaurants and on public transportation were also friendlier and more polite than in some other cities in the country. Even if they were "fake" and did not mean it, it felt so much better. It made me feel happier and more connected to people.

This comparison of cultures was a complicated topic. What were the societal norms, how could you comply with them, and what could you do if you breached them? What was rude?

What we reduced it down to, from our end, was how we felt when we were in different cities and countries. We agreed that the more people smiled, the more comfortable we felt. If people were polite and helpful, we experienced more joy. If people barked at us, pushed us, refused to answer questions, belittled us, we felt simultaneously demeaned and angry. If people used their bureaucratic power to cause us unnecessary delay and complications, we felt disrespected. If we were not fully aware of the cultural norms and made a mistake, we appreciated it when we were given some leeway and forgiveness. We felt responsible to try to make our travel experiences more positive. We acknowledged that we had to try not to be rude from the perspective of the people in the places we visited.

My friendship with Helene was a gift to me. It seemed that, unlike the people we watched on media, and those we sometimes experienced in our lives, we were able to agree, disagree, and agree to disagree without being rude to one another. One thing we both acknowledged was that we had to try to be mannerly in all of our dealings since we could not control what others did or do. If we all took that approach, maybe we could turn things around, and leave the stragglers behind. Even when we did not achieve perfection, we could remain aware and renew our efforts. We remembered the song we learned years ago which ended with "Kindness begins with me."

At the end of our time at the diner, Helene gave me a check. She knew that I was struggling financially, and she wanted to ease my burden. My grandson had special needs and needed some special tutoring, as well as some expensive equipment to help him learn at school. She knew that I was frustrated because it was difficult for me to help him given my other financial responsibilities. She told me that the check was for me to use as I saw fit. I did not want to accept it, but I did not want to be rude in not accepting it. She told me that it would please her for me to have it, but she did not want to be rude in making me accept it.

She told me that all of our discussions about civility and kindness had led to this moment. She reasoned that we cannot fix the world, but we can try to help each other. She explained that given her financial situation, it was not a burden upon her at all. After all, she declared, "charity begins at home," meaning our first responsibility is for the needs of our family and friends. I did not like the word charity, nor did she, but I accepted her kindness because I knew that I would reciprocate in my own way.

Chapter Five

Youth Obsessed, Youth Possessed

"To lose confidence in one's body is to lose confidence in oneself."

—Simone de Beauvoir

"My face carries all my memories. Why would I erase them?"

—Diane von Furstenberg

Nora was my conscience, my influencer, my barometer, my measuring stick, especially for all things which emboldened women. Whenever we talked, it was as if I received a shot of adrenaline, and could go on and do those things I was most afraid of. Her view of the world was my catalyst.

We met forty years ago when I was a journalist, and she was a photographer. We worked for the same magazine. At the time, I remember thinking that Nora should have been the model instead of the photographer, her looks were so striking. She was tall, naturally thin, with porcelain skin, green eyes, blonde long hair, a strong jawline and high cheekbones. She walked and sat like a dancer, with excellent posture and grace. She wore little make up, and adorned herself with the same few pieces of well chosen jewelry. Her clothes were understated and tailored. She mostly wore pieces which were either all black or all beige. She wore stylish but comfortable flat shoes. She never carried a handbag. She did everything with subtle style, discipline and moderation.

She was one of those women who seemed aware of her beauty and the advantages it gave her, without letting her appearance rule her life or overly consume her time. To her, it was an advantage, similar to having innate musical ability. It was given to her, but she largely ignored it when she could. She did not notice it slowly fade like watching water boil. She was a serious photographer, and used her aesthetic ability to create superior photographs, and to create her own personal style. Her appearance was part of her creative effort, although her true gift was making everything she did seem effortless.

When we were in our early seventies, we were still working, but for ourselves. I was doing an article as a freelancer about how difficult it continued to be for women to age in our society, especially regarding our appearances. She was working as a photographer, also as a freelancer, but was mostly doing creative pieces to enter into shows. She had made significant money in her early sixties, modeling to represent the older woman in magazines and on television. She was no longer modeling as she had "aged out" of the older model opportunities. I decided to interview her because in my view she made for an interesting subject. She was someone who gazed at others through her lens, and then experienced being gazed at as a model in her senior years. I was confident that her perspective on society's continued obsession with youth and beauty would be compelling.

I went to her apartment for the interview. She lived alone in the West Village of New York City in a rent stabilized apartment which she had occupied for fifty years. It was on a leafy street with low buildings in an elegant, relatively quiet neighborhood. She had a working fireplace with a white, carved, marble mantle. She displayed some objects from her travels, including African masks, and Turkish rugs, and had some well-cared-for plants, but it was mostly a minimalist, clean space. The floors were well-worn wood, the ceilings were high, the walls were white, and the only framed pictures on the walls were some of her black and white photographs. Her counters throughout the apartment were empty. Everything was placed in closets or in USM modern storage cabinets. It was restful to look at her apartment, much as it was restful to look at her.

We sat in her second bedroom, which served as her office. It, too, was neat and uncluttered, except for a bookshelf which contained a few Buddhas she had collected in Asia, and some art and photography books. The space was defined by a large window which overlooked tree tops and let in a lot of light. We sat on opposite sides of a Chesterfield style beige leather sofa, like bookends. I taped our conversation and took notes.

I asked her how her youthful beauty had impacted her when she was younger. She said: "From my first memories, I can remember that most people commented on what a beautiful child, and then young woman, I was. I knew that to them it was something good, but I did not truly understand their adulation. It seemed that my teachers treated me exceptionally well, my classmates mostly wanted to befriend me, and boys, from an early age, seemed excessively interested in me. My mother was a staunch feminist, which is probably what saved me from developing excessive worry about my appearance in an effort to continue the admiration I would have felt was my due. She told me that I had an advantage in being physically attractive, but that being a kind person, and the development of my brain and talents, were the most important elements for a happy life.

I was shy by nature. I preferred taking photographs and reading to spending time with others. That is why becoming a professional photographer was such a bonus for me. I could be an introvert, and still function in society. I did not have to be the center of attention the way the models were. I was approached many times when I was younger to model. My parents were asked frequently to allow me to model as well. They refused to permit me to do it, as they thought I would live a material, fast life with drugs, and danger from sexual predators. More importantly, they thought, philosophically, that the emphasis on beauty was misplaced. I had no desire to model at that time. It would have been torture for me.

Once I started my career in photography, my appearance gave me an advantage, especially with men. Men wanted to hire me to be around me. They equated my appearance with my work, which allowed me in the door, and then I proved to them that I worked hard on my talent.

There was a negative side to being what was considered beautiful throughout my young life. Many girls, and then women, were jealous of me. Sometimes I was not hired for jobs if the woman was doing the hiring. Some boys, and then men, wanted to be with me primarily because of their egos. They thought that I would make good 'arm candy,' which would benefit them. On balance, I cannot say whether my 'beauty' helped me or hurt me in all of the most important ways. It was simply my reality."

I asked her why she never married or had children. She said:

"I have had a difficult time finding love, in part, because of what men think of my beauty. Some men were intimidated by it and were not able to approach me or befriend me. Many men I dated did not see the real me. They only saw with their eyes. In addition, I was extremely career oriented. I never thought much about having children. It was not my priority. Like some men, my work came first, and many men did not like that quality in me. I preferred the urban environment of New York City and did not want to end up living in the suburbs in a house, where the work I wanted was hard to find. I wanted freedom to pursue my profession and my creativity. I thought that a man might interfere with that. Some tried to, but those relationships did not last. Whenever one of my relationships ended, my friends and family would tell me that I would have no trouble finding someone else because I was attractive. It is true that I could always find someone, but never the right one for me, ultimately.

There was a fear that I had, too, when I was younger. If a man chose me because of my "beauty," what would happen to that love when my beauty faded? I did not want to be one of those women who married, had children, built their entire world around their husband, and then, when their beauty faded, were no longer useful and were replaced. I did not want to spend my time worrying about that eventuality, or visiting plastic surgeons and dermatologists to try to fight time. I did not want my life to be defined by a man's gaze."

I asked her if she thought that she would ever marry. She replied:

"I suppose anything can happen in life. Gloria Steinem, one of our favorite and most famous feminists, married at age sixty-six. On the other hand, there are less men than women at our age, so I do not know if the shrinking pool will impact on my chance to find the right person. I do feel the need for companionship more at our age than I ever did before. I do not rule anything out."

I questioned her about why she started to model in her early sixties, and what it was like for her. She said:

"When I entered my sixties, I started to panic about whether I would have enough money in my old age. While I was making a living with my photography, it was a relatively meager one. I had not saved enough, and knew I needed one last push to fill my savings coffers.

Through my magazine work, I met some people who wanted me to be a model to represent older women. At that point in my life, I had overcome some of my shyness, and took a practical view that I could earn relatively easy money doing it. I took advantage of that opportunity for five years until I started to look too old and did not want plastic surgery, botox or fillers, which they told me I had to have in order to continue.

During the period that I modeled, I felt that I had lost a bit of my soul for several reasons. One was that we were selling to older women that it was fine to age, if they looked like me. But even I did not look like me. It took a whole team of experts to create me, and an enormous amount of time. They dyed my hair a special color of gray, which looked as though it was realistic, but was anything but. It took hours of putting in highlights and lowlights to achieve that effect. The make-up artist was a genius. She took away many of my lines and spots, and achieved smooth contouring. She used colors to give me a 'youthful glow.' I wore 'head to toe' Spanx to give me a taut look. They lifted my sagging breasts with push up bras and tape. The photographer knew the tricks, as I did, to make someone look younger. The angles she used, the light and shadow she played with, were employed to make me look extraordinary, while tricking the eye that it was all natural.

My body was no longer 'perfect.' After the photographs were taken, they photoshopped them so that my stomach bulge no longer showed. They edited away some signs of extra, saggy skin, from my neck down to my knees. My hands were made to appear a younger version of what they actually were, while still leaving in some spots and lines for realism. People who saw my print and television advertisements loved my image and I became a popular 'older' model.

This did not please me necessarily. It was a purely mercenary endeavor. I was a version of a Stepford Wife, a robot, in my case created by the advertising world, or a Barbie doll, and I knew it.

Another reason my years as a model disturbed me is that I did not think that the 'bionic' me which they had created was more attractive than the real me. The message they were giving women is that signs of aging are ugly, and we must minimize them. My modeling and letting them transform me contributed to that negative view of aging. At the time I rationalized my decision to model. I reasoned that there were so few older models like me, and that I was a pioneer breaking a barrier. I convinced myself that it was a first step, the way the ads for underwear with some overweight women were a first step toward body diversity in advertising. Not all of the prejudices could be undone at once, I whispered to myself.

A negative by-product of my modeling time was that I became more self conscious in real life. I began to wear sunglasses and hats in public, as if I were a celebrity ducking from the paparazzi. I became afraid that if people recognized me from my print and television ads, they would think to themselves that I was a fraud, and that I did not look like that at all. In some sense I was ashamed that I did not look like that. Before I modeled, I was perfectly comfortable with the aging process. After I became a model, I felt that I was a specimen, open for inspection by the public. I was terrified of being attacked and shamed on social media. All my years of resisting using my appearance as my work was slowly becoming undone along with some of the confidence which my parents had instilled in me. I knew I needed to get back to a healthier viewpoint.

After five years, even a team of experts could not make me into the woman they wanted me to be for their ads. They said I could continue if I were willing to undergo some treatments and surgeries. At that point, I had reached my savings goal, and wanted to turn my efforts toward more artistic and creative endeavors. I was grateful for the money, but not for how that profession made me feel. I was relieved that I could let that phase of my life end.

After I stopped modeling, I began to take pictures of older people, mostly women, in my everyday life and during my travels. As a photographer, I found the beauty in the bend of their bodies, the contours of their wrinkles, the light in their eyes, the joy in their smiles. I wanted to make up for the fake images of older people that we see in advertisements, and which I had been a part of. I wanted to get away from the shaming of women. I had a few shows of these photographs at galleries, and some interviews about my work. I felt that I was slowly returning to the self which I could admire.

When I had an opportunity to speak about the photographs, I mentioned my observations. I told the audiences that women were deified if we were born with good looks. We were deified if we retained those looks naturally into old age. We were deified if we had plastic surgery and treatments which looked like we did not do anything to ourselves. We were ashamed if we were born with a face or body which the society at that time did not consider beautiful. We were ashamed if we did not age well. We were ashamed if we tried to hold onto our youth by getting surgeries and treatments which made us unattractive because they were not done properly, or our faces and bodies did not react well to it."

I told Nora that I was proud of what she had accomplished with her photography. I said that I understood why she needed to be practical to make money with something she did not feel comfortable with in order to insure her financial future so that she could support herself. I mentioned that many women whom I knew personally, and whom I interviewed professionally, had admitted to me that they had allowed others to shame them about their appearance throughout their lives. They discussed with me the hours that they wasted thinking about how to make themselves more attractive and engaging in treatments with the hope of doing so. They resented the time spent wondering if they only lost ten or twenty pounds, or if their skin was unlined, that this or that would happen for them. They resented all of the money that they spent on "beauty" which they could have used for their families and for more education, interesting trips, and cultural events. Nora replied:

"I appreciate your support and insights. Media, advertising and the entertainment industry perpetuate our society's obsession with youth and beauty. I tried to do some simple things in my life to keep it all in perspective. I spent as little time on my appearance as possible. I would lay out my clothes the night before so I would not have to think much about it. I wore interchangeable, solid colors to make multiple outfits out of a few pieces. Once I could order clothes, beauty products and makeup online, I did that. I dressed for both comfort and style. I exercised each day for my health. I took good care of myself by eating healthy foods and going for doctor's checkups, but I did not spend much more time on my appearance than men do.

I remember that there were two major decisions I made about my appearance which were difficult for me, and I know were difficult for other women too. The first, which I made in my fifties, was to give up wearing high heeled shoes. They were sexy, they made you walk a certain way, and they made your legs look better, or so we were brainwashed. I was on my feet a lot as a photographer. My back was starting to ache. My doctors told me that I was ruining my feet and back. In truth, it was a decision which was made for me. I am embarrassed to admit that I still admire women who can continue to wear high heels at advanced ages. It is irrational, I know. It is similar to women who admire those who were able to give birth vaginally instead of by caesarean section. Their bodies made that choice for them. It was not some strength or weakness. We are brainwashed against ourselves.

The second decision was whether or not to continue to dye my hair blonde, or any other color for that matter. My friends had extremely strong views on the matter. One camp thought that dying hair was not healthy, that it was too expensive, and that authentic, natural hair was better. The other camp believed that not dying your hair was making a statement to the world that you no longer cared about your appearance, which was a decision to be avoided at all costs. Also, they argued, people would discriminate against you more because of age, especially in the workplace. Having gray hair was not an option if you wanted to survive professionally.

I personally did not attach any of those views to my decision. I was tired of taking the time to dye it, I could no longer justify the expense in light of all the other things I wanted to do with that money, and as a photographer and artist, I decided I could figure out a way to make it look good. All of my minimalist decisions freed up so much time for me. I do not regret any of them.

How do we feel confident in our own skin, as women, literally and figuratively, when we are getting so many messages which make it hard for us to like ourselves? We are social animals by nature, and we want and need the approval of others. I think there comes a time in every woman's life when she has to decide what is most important to her, and how to achieve it. Perhaps that is our greatest strength as we age, and what makes us truly beautiful.

My life has always been my work of art. I stopped listening to what the society I was born into told me was important and the right thing to do, at an early age. My parents gave me the confidence to do so. Not everybody has the advantage of that support, but you can raise yourself, eventually. Society told me that my beauty was important. Society told me that if I was beautiful, I could not be intelligent. Society told me that I should get married and have children. Society told me that photography was not a way to make a good living. Society told me that I should do everything in my power not to look my age, and that youth is better than old age. Society told me that aging is ugly.

It is not a question of my having been rebellious. It was an early realization that one is on earth for a limited period of time, and you have to do what your heart tells you to do. I knew early on that marriage and children were not for me. Not all women are made for that, just like not all men are made to be good providers. People tried to shame me about that decision. They called me immature, selfish, and even unstable. I knew in my heart that none of those adjectives applied, although it did tie me up in knots for a while. It takes great strength to live the life you want to live.

On a more superficial level, I knew the way I wanted to look. When I was in high school, I tried to copy the way that other girls appeared, even buying the exact items they wore, whether they were meant for me or not. I was taller than most of the girls, and some of the boys, so I would hunch over so as not to stand out. Once in college, I found my own style and how I wanted to present myself to the world. I changed my posture, and came into my own. It went on from there.

Now that I am in my seventies, I feel more free than ever to express who I am. I stopped caring what others think, especially about my appearance, to an ever greater degree. I try to be kind, but I am no longer seeking to please others to the detriment of myself. I feel wiser and more centered. I know how to expend my energies better. I know what looks good and feels good.

I appreciate being older and healthy. I am thrilled that I do not have a period. I appreciate that I have money in the bank, and more time to spend on my creative pursuits. I value my friendships which have lasted into my old age. I am grateful for senior discounts at museums, movies, cultural events and transportation."

I told Nora that she was blessed not only with great beauty inside and out, but an attitude which gave her opportunities to continue to grow and achieve for this latter part of her life. I asked her if she had any challenges which she at some point did not think she could overcome, but eventually did. She said:

"When I was in my fifties, I was diagnosed with breast cancer. I had radiation and chemotherapy, and it was dormant until my sixties, when it came back. It was not necessary for me to have a mastectomy, although I did lose my hair both times. After the second diagnosis, for a number of years, I lived in fear every day. I was afraid that the cancer would return and spread. When my fears became crippling, in that I suffered a deep depression, I went to a therapist for a few years. After counseling, I was able to use the disease as a catalyst for living my life in the best way I could for me.

Ironically, unlike many other women, I was not particularly disturbed over losing my hair. I bought some good wigs, and enjoyed playing with different images of myself. I did not lose my breasts, so I did not have to cope with that body change, and, honestly, I do not know how I would have reacted. It was not my appearance which caused me concern. It was my fear that I would not be able to take care of myself, that I would be in constant pain, and that I would not be able to work. I tried not to think about the ultimate fear of dying. What depressed me was how I was going to live with it."

After the interview was over, we planned our next outing to a photography exhibit. I always looked forward to spending time with her and hearing her viewpoints on life. Five years later, Nora ended up in a nursing home. She had a form of dementia, and could no longer take care of herself. I went to visit her every few months. I asked the nurse in charge of the floor where Nora was living how she was doing. She told me that her memory was getting worse, but that she had a gentleman friend who lived across the hall, and spent many hours during the day with her. He was wheelchair bound, but his memory was intact.

On one of my visits, I met him. He and Nora were holding hands, and sitting in her room. He had been a dentist, and was a cultured and interesting man. He told me that he and Nora were in love, and that their companionship was keeping both of them alive. He shared with me that although she suffered some cognitive impairment, the insights she was able to share were interesting and unique. As he gazed at her, he told me that he could look at her all day, and it made life beautiful for him. He was hoping that she would agree to marry him.

Chapter Six

When Queen Bees Sting

"No one can make you feel inferior without your consent."

—Eleanor Roosevelt

"Other women are not my competition. I stand with them,
not against them."

At an annual convention of a professional women's organization, whose mission was, in part, the advancement of women in society, I attended a class session on women bullying other women at work. A portion of the discussion was about the Queen Bee syndrome, which had been defined as women with power who treat subordinate women worse than men because of their gender. Much of the meeting centered on the myth of female solidarity in the workplace, and the torturous bind of women needing to depend on other women, but being in competition with them in a negative way, whether they were bosses, subordinates or co-workers. We all agreed that it was painful to acknowledge that despite the advances accomplished because of the feminist movement, in its many generational phases, there was still work to do with women bullying other women at work. We needed to find ways to improve the workplace for women going forward, and it was not just about unequal pay, the glass ceiling, and the lack of affordable child care alternatives, although those factors likely contributed to the women-on-women aggression.

After the session, I met with my mentor, Karen, with whom I reconnected each year at the organization's conventions. She had been my boss ten years ago, and because of her support of me, was responsible, in large measure, for my professional advancement. Even after I left the company where we worked together, she continued to provide me with guidance and advice in my subsequent positions. I helped her professionally while I worked for her, and thereafter in terms of networking and information. We recognized that our relationship was a positive example of how women can creatively mentor, collaborate, connect, nurture and support one another. Our feminine wiring for those things had worked to both of our advantages.

What was preventing more of those relationships from occurring at work? Karen and I started to talk about our memories of "mean girl" behavior, also known as relational aggression, as we were growing up, and how that informed our reactions later on. That had been one of the exercises in the class we had just attended. Some of the topics we discussed were jealousy, envy and competition between women in school, as adults in the community, and in the workplace, and how we dealt with it.

Karen grew up in an extremely competitive environment. In high school, in order to be friendly with the most popular, powerful girls, one had to be beautiful, smart, accomplished, and wealthy. She recalled that the women's movement had "helped" in that just being beautiful and wealthy was not enough, but now the competition was extended to every aspect of your life.

You had to have some special skill, and get into the most prestigious college. It was similar to the requirements being increased for winning beauty pageants.

She remembered that she made an "executive" decision early on in her life. Karen was not interested in being in a clique or actively participating in the competitions between the girls, except for doing well in school. She had different friends for each of her interests and had friends who were in different cliques. Somehow she managed to make her own arrangement which suited her. There were a few "floaters" like her, and some who were loners.

She loved to be invited to other people's homes to see how they lived, from a sociological and somewhat detached perspective. Karen was deeply interested in people's stories, and was a good listener, but she somehow did not feel a part of any of it. She had numbed herself. She liked to spend time by herself reading, and dreamed of a bigger world beyond the pettiness she observed from the materialists, manipulators, gossip spreaders and excluders. Karen was considered one of the "nice" girls who tried not to talk about other girls behind their backs, or to steal their boyfriends, or to sabotage them in any way. In fact, she was usually quite helpful to her female peers, and to her peers in general. Karen was considered "safe" to be friendly with, to confide in, and had honed her collaboration skills early on.

Karen believed in empowering herself and other girls, even then. She did not have as strong a need for acceptance as some of her peers, which was unusual at that age. Karen did not recall being picked on much, although there were instances when people made insulting remarks about her body, her clothes, and sometimes her projects at school. She had one friend she spent a lot of time with, who was her support system, and she mostly focused on her schoolwork to get good grades and move on. Karen had a job after school, so she did not have a lot of extra time, and she did not start to date until college. She acknowledged that she had retreated into a form of passivity and withdrew from the competition. She remained somewhat invisible.

Karen recalled that although she tried to meld into the woodwork, she had no problem defending other girls who were being picked on. She was not afraid of the repercussions, because for her there would be few. Karen did not care if she was excluded or shunned. She was close to her mother and sisters, and to her one close friend, and had them for support. She had a few teachers who served as mentors. She felt relatively protected.

I told her that I had not removed myself from the competition, and had been deeply hurt by what I had perceived as the betrayals of certain friends in high school. My mother was divorced, she worked all the time, and we did not have a lot of money. I was sensitive and needy at that time. Therefore, my friends became all important to me, and I relied on them to be my nurturing parents, which was a role they could not fulfill. I was part of a group, and I do recall being excluded from certain parties and gatherings. I remembered being teased about my teeth, which needed fixing, and my clothes, which were not the most stylish or of the highest quality as money was tight in my household.

There was one boy who was interested in me in high school. We started to date, and he became my boyfriend. My best friend flirted with him to get him to like her. She then arranged to be around him quite a bit. It made me uncomfortable, but I was not certain what was going on. He eventually dropped me and asked her out. She was not really interested in him. She just wanted to show me that she could have him, and once she did, she started to go out with someone else. I could never feel the same about her, and we ceased being friends.

After that, I became more discerning about which girls I would let into my inner circle, and was on high alert about the ones who would stab you in the back to get a boyfriend, or who would sabotage you in your school classes or other activities. If I saw that they were gossiping about other girls, or engaging in other mean behaviors, such as eye-rolling or body-scanning other girls, I crossed them off my mental list of confidantes and friends. I stayed away from the girls who said cruel things, freezed other girls out, or were jealous of anyone else's successes. Sometimes I made mistakes, and did not realize that another girl was a "mean girl" until it was too late.

We talked about how all of this early "training" impacted our experiences as adults. We both were married with children. We shared how the one-upmanship continued into our adult lives. I lived in a suburban community, while Karen lived in the city. We discussed how our friendships with other women through our children sometimes revolved around competing about our children, our husbands, our home or apartment, our cars, our clothes, our jewelry, our vacations, and even our shortcomings.

As full-time working women, we experienced competition amongst ourselves, with part-time working women, and with those women who did not work outside the home. There was a contest, sometimes subtle, and sometimes not, about who was the best mother or who had the best career. We experienced mostly covert competition and indirect aggression. Many women were trying to legitimize their choices at the expense of true friendship. There was a lot of self-hatred revolving around what was chosen and what was given up in order to manage our respective families and lives.

Karen shared a negative experience she had with another mother, whom she thought was her friend. Karen told the other mother, in confidence, that she was applying to a certain school for one of her children which had few slots and took only one child from the middle school that both of their children attended. Karen's child had her heart set on going to that particular high school, because of its emphasis on science, and Karen's friend knew it. The other mother, who did not know of the opportunity, quickly applied, and got her own child into the school, although her child had no interest in science. Karen's child was not accepted.

If Karen had not told the other mother, she might have had that slot for her child. The competition for schools in the city was fierce, and sharing information, even with a so-called friend, could have its down side. The other mother constantly pitted her daughter against Karen's daughter, sometimes going after opportunities just to try to win, rather than because her daughter cared about the activity. It made Karen sad, and she vowed to try to behave differently.

Karen told me that she made great efforts to collaborate with women who did not work full time or outside the home. She wanted to foster mutual respect and to make meaningful connections. With a few stay-at-home moms, Karen took care of their children along with her own on the weekends to give them a break, and they would help her out during the week with carpooling to different activities. Those arrangements fit her personality. She found a way for everybody to win.

I asked Karen how she managed to create that environment wherever she went. She said, wryly, that, because she always took herself out of the competition, for better or worse, she was not seen as a threat. She was not the best looking, richest, or most accomplished, so she generally was not an object of too much envy or jealousy. She did well enough to be interesting, without being someone on a pedestal who needed to be brought down, or who had to bring down others to stay at the top. Her humility and lack of "aggression" made her palatable to other women and men. That was the secret of her success. But, as she acknowledged, she did not get the very top jobs, although she was certainly qualified for them.

I shared with Karen that in my suburban community, if you had the money to join the country club and could afford to go out to certain restaurants, you could have entry into a certain crowd. The women who were married to the most successful men were at the top of the heap. Social acceptance and approval were exceedingly important to that group.

The few women who were uber successful at work and commuted into the City were largely out of the loop in every sense of the word. I worked so much and had so many responsibilities with the family, that I orbited outside of all of that hierarchy, although I was aware of it, as were my children, in a subtle way. It was similar to high school, but in some sense worse as there were more levels to compete about. Some of the mothers orchestrated friendships for their children based on these hierarchies, and later tried to loosely arrange marriages for them based on social class. All of this is nothing new, but it seemed as though we should have outgrown some of it.

Competition sometimes took an ugly turn right in our neighborhoods. I recalled a situation where families lived on a particular street in our community, and often got together for neighborhood barbeques and other events. One of my friends who lived on that street, Barbara, noticed that another woman, Rita, who was also married, was spending an inordinate amount of time trying to talk to her husband on each occasion. Barbara was friendly with Rita, and they had been to each other's homes many times.

Rita's husband was having some difficulties being a provider, in that his business was not doing well, and Rita was extremely materialistic. She openly expressed to all who would listen that she was not happy with her current circumstances. Barbara's husband was a successful entrepreneur. It was clear that Rita wanted to find a new situation. As she had given up her own career, a man was her only way to achieve the lifestyle she wanted. Eventually Rita and Barbara's husband had an affair, and both couples obtained a divorce. Barbara developed an alcohol problem for a time to cope with the situation, and the children of both families had a lot of difficulties adjusting to the new reality. Eventually, Barbara was able to come to terms with what had happened. It helped her that she had maintained her career throughout her marriage. This was another example of a woman vying for limited resources. As might be expected, Barbara's ex-husband's marriage with Rita did not last. Rita found an even richer man in the neighborhood, who also left his wife for her.

We discussed that women competed primarily with each other at every juncture of our lives. The old adage that women dressed for each other, in every sense, is probably still true. We acknowledged how much women needed each other, but, in many instances, failed to support one another adequately. The media promotes "cat fights" between women, with less emphasis on solidarity and community. Good feelings between women does not make for interesting entertainment in our culture, but was an aspiration we both embraced. We did have many examples of positive experiences with women at each stage of our lives, so we had not given up. But somehow the bad experiences left more indelible marks on our psyches.

Then we turned to what went on between women in the workplace. I told Karen that having had the privilege of working for her earlier in my career set me on a path to do the right thing for other women. Unfortunately, all women were not like Karen. I asked her if she had experienced any bullying from other women in her career. She shared several stories.

She said that early on in her career, she had a Queen Bee boss named Ellen. Karen had been hired by Ellen's supervisor, Walt. Karen had graduated from Yale University, as did Walt, and her boss Ellen was intimidated by that. Karen was accustomed to succeeding by working hard, and learning quickly. She was not prepared for the palace intrigue. The Queen Bee boss went to an average college, and had worked her way up from the secretarial pool to a senior level position at the company. She would not teach Karen how to do anything, withheld information from her, and left Karen out of strategic meetings and conferences. Ellen wanted to maintain her position, and wanted to make certain that Karen did not have the tools to outshine her.

Karen said that when she first started working, she had a "weak" personality and was not as assertive as she should have been. The Queen Bee took advantage of her position, and of Karen's personality, to harass her on a daily basis. She set Karen up to fail. On many occasions, she berated Karen's work in front of other co-workers. Karen recalled that she went to the bathroom, and burst into tears, several times. At meetings, when Karen voiced her opinion, Ellen often made noises of disgust, crossed her arms and rolled her eyes. She made it clear to all that she did not respect Karen, although the underlying reason for her behavior was because she was intimidated by Karen's intelligence, work ethic, and honorable behavior.

The Queen Bee had a drinking problem. Sometimes she would come back from lunch, after having had a few drinks too many, burst into Karen's office with a list of demands, scream at her, and berate her for not working more quickly. Karen had eaten her sandwich from home at her desk so as not to waste any time. The Queen Bee would often say to Karen, that with Karen's first-rate education, she should have been performing better.

Karen did not realize that her relationship with her boss was not about Karen's work performance, but was about the fact that there were very few high level positions for women in the firm and competition was fierce. Ellen was used to being the only high level woman in the group, and she wanted to keep it that way.

After a few months of working for the Queen Bee, Karen started to lose. She lost weight, lost hair, lost sleep, lost confidence, and lost her direction. After a year of suffering, she went to Walt, in confidence, and asked him to move her to a different unit. She was lucky that they had another place for her within the company. When she saw the Queen Bee at firm functions after the transfer, the Queen Bee was as sweet to Karen as could be. They were no longer in competition, so it did not hurt her to be kind. Ellen had eliminated the threat and had a new victim working for her.

Karen remembered another Queen Bee she had worked for named Sybil. The woman preferred her male bosses and male subordinates, and virtually ignored Karen. The Queen Bee talked sports with the men, offered them rides home, socialized with them on nights and weekends, and gave them promotions and better assignments. Sybil acted like an imitation stereotypical man. She drank hard liquor, used swear words frequently, bet on sports, and had a hard, no-nonsense exterior. Sybil was extremely tough, and believed that if her male bosses and underlings saw her as no different from them, they would give her more respect. If Karen ever showed any signs of weakness, the Queen Bee would tell her to stop complaining, stop sniveling, and outwork the men the way that she did in order to get ahead. Sybil said you had to show men that you were not like other women to succeed.

Sybil used many high school techniques to retain her power. She would alternate between screaming at Karen and the few other women, and icing them out. Sometimes she would take assignments away from them and give them to the men as a form of shaming them. She would ridicule Karen by imitating her voice, or making fun of aspects of her work. She used derogatory names for Karen in front of other people such as "airhead," which is a stupid or simple-minded person, ditsy, emotional, hormonal, hysterical, and irrational. She referred to Karen as breathless, like Marilyn Monroe. Karen had bleached blonde hair, so the comparison to Marilyn Monroe had a nasty edge to it. All of the words were obviously meant to demean her and to have people see Karen in a certain "less than" light.

That Queen Bee, like many others, had given up her entire personal life in order to get ahead. Her personal life was her work life. Sybil wanted Karen to do the same. Karen did not think that it was the proper balance for her, and she had children at home. The Queen Bee was not going to let her have that balance. Sybil told Karen that she had to make sacrifices to succeed, and so would Karen. Karen did not stay in that job for very long.

I asked Karen if she had any other stories. She told me that she was close to a co-worker named Jane for several years. They often had lunch together, and shared much personal information about their lives. Karen decided to apply for an MBA degree program as a night student when her children were school age. She thought that it would give her an advantage at work, and the company would pay for it.

Jane began to behave differently toward Karen when she learned that Karen had been accepted into the MBA program. Rather than giving her support, she told Karen that it was a mistake to spend so little time with her family, and that her marriage and children would suffer as a result of her selfish decision. Karen had not asked her opinion, and felt that her unsolicited advice was unwanted and mean. Karen had to use her lunch time to study, so they spent less and less time together. Karen was not sorry, because she felt that Jane was too judgmental and not encouraging enough.

Jane felt threatened by Karen's decision. She lacked Karen's confidence, and did not believe that she could manage a husband, children and home along with a full-time job and part-time graduate program. Karen was able to multitask and do all of these things, albeit with anxiety and many months of doubt, but she ultimately succeeded. Jane was invited to Karen's graduation ceremony. Jane said she had other plans and could not attend. Jane lost a friend and ally at work because of her own insecurities and her feelings of jealousy and competition which did not have to divide them. Nonetheless, when Jane applied for a different job within the company and asked Karen to serve as a reference, Karen gladly gave her a glowing review because she was a good worker, just not a good friend.

Karen asked me to share some of my work stories. I remembered how I was one of a handful of professional women in a department. The support staff, including the secretaries, were all female. No matter how friendly, polite and kind I behaved, the support staff would always help the men in the department first. I analyzed my behavior to determine if I was giving off a superior air, or if I was doing something to irritate them. I spoke about it with the other professional women, and they shared that they experienced the same treatment. We know that women often do not like to work for other women. It was a cultural thing. We just did not know how to change it. We thought that over time if more professional women worked in the department, the situation might change. But more women working together does not always work well.

I recalled a situation where a female boss went out of her way to make my life more difficult. She had 24/7 nannies to help her at home. At that point, I had a husband and young children. She would contact me on a Friday night, after I arrived home, and give me an assignment due Monday which would take up my time over the weekend. This was not a one time situation or an emergency. Her work life melded into her personal life. She wanted me to commit 24/7 to the job. In addition, she would text me about her personal matters at night and during the weekend, and expect me to immediately respond.

When I did not make myself completely available to her outside of work hours, she found ways to punish me. She would give me an extremely difficult travel schedule for that week. Other times, when she knew I had plans to go away for the weekend with my family, she set up the schedule so that I could not leave with them. She took away my privileges to work from home on occasion if she wanted to wreak havoc with my schedule. She wanted to show me that she could "own" me at all times.

Another boss had expected me to go to lunch with her every day. She was earning twice my salary, so that was not difficult for her. I wanted to bring my lunch to save money. Also, as the younger person in the office, I had to work longer hours to prove myself, and wanted to work through lunch. When I told her that it was difficult for me to go to lunch with her for these reasons, she became angry with me, and started to criticize my work more. My husband told me that if it would keep the peace, we would budget a special lunch money fund to keep my boss happy. After I did that, and went to lunch with her again, the boss was pleased with me. This was another instance where the personal became political.

One Queen Bee boss resented me because I had a husband, and he had a high paying job. I had healthy children. We lived in the suburbs. She lived alone in the city in a luxury building in an all-white apartment she hired an interior designer to decorate. She wore designer clothing, luxury jewelry and furs to work. I did not. After I was hired for a certain professional position, she started to give me menial work, such as getting her coffee from Starbucks, cleaning her office desk and bookshelves, and some of her personal chores, like picking up her dry cleaning or picking up her food for lunch, which were outside the job description. I was not hired as her personal assistant. When I complained, the Queen Bee tried to make it seem as though I was spoiled and entitled, and did not work as much as my coworkers. I worked as hard as they did at work, and worked a second shift with my family after work. She made fun of the fact that sometimes, for my commute, I would take a taxicab from the train to the office for convenience, instead of a bus or subway.

One day there was a heavy snowstorm. The taxicab could not get through the streets to get me to the office. I called in and said that I could not make it. I offered to do my work from home, which I did. My boss lived a few blocks from the office and could walk there. Some other employees who lived close by were able to make it in. With the Queen Bee leading the charge, I was attacked the next day for not coming to work. The Queen Bee said that I was lazy and that I pampered myself to the detriment of others. She set it up so that my coworkers were against me. They were afraid of her and allowed her to bully me so that they would not have to absorb any of the flack. I left that job as soon as I found a new one.

In another office setting, my female coworkers liked to go out on Friday night for drinks. It was a mostly female work environment. I had a long commute, a family waiting for me at home, and I did not like to drink. They also did a sports lottery in the office. I was not interested in sports, nor did I enjoy gambling. I am a museum, ballet, opera, classical music kind of gal. It is important to fit into the culture where you work, and clearly I did not.

My coworkers, particularly the other women, thought I was snotty, or that there was something not right about me. They made fun of my appearance, my personality and my interests. I made no attempt to fit in. I just wanted to do my work and go home. It seemed as if I had to be similar in order to be well liked. They started to exclude me from their conversations at work, and talked behind my back. Conversations would cease once I walked into their offices. It became uncomfortable since I enjoyed having collegial relationships with coworkers. Eventually I left that job for a better one.

There were so many stories we could tell each other, some positive and some negative, about women interacting with one another. What Karen and I realized in the telling was how many anxieties girls/women have throughout their lives which often pit women against other women. In the early years it is the need to fit into a group and for social approval. Later it is about finding the right mate. Then there are concerns about having children. If we have children too early we could ruin our careers. If we wait to have children, our fertility diminishes over time. Will we be ostracized if we do not want children? We are in competition for limited resources with love, marriage, work, and family. That is when jealousy, envy and competition can enter the equation.

We read and discussed different theories about why women aggress against each other. Some say that, because of the expanded opportunities for women, we have competition on more fronts now. Some say it is because we are vying for limited resources, and if there are more positions in the workplace for women at higher levels, there will be less competition and more opportunity for mutual respect and connection. We agreed that if there are more mentoring programs for women, there will be constructive ways to avoid bullying situations, especially since involving human resources departments does not always work to a woman's advantage. For heterosexual women, if there are more men available, there will be less competition.

How to achieve that circumstance is anyone's guess. If there is more and better daycare at a reasonable cost, there will be an important societal support for women in place. If there are more educational opportunities for children, mothers will be less inclined to vie against one another.

Some postulate that women have historically been interested in protecting and getting resources for their own families, and that the myth of female solidarity is just that, a myth.

We tried to analyze how we could make the situation better for women. We thought that an education and media campaign about women learning to respect and accept each other's differences and similarities would be helpful. We do not have to be doing the same things at the same time in order to be supportive to one another. We do not have to let the media get away with portraying women as constantly cat fighting and against one another. We have to send out a message of lifting one another up.

Our organization works on legislation and other means to improve the lives of women. If we keep working together on these issues, perhaps we can get away from the backstabbing, the undermining and the self-hatred which characterize some of our interactions with one another. We can celebrate each other's accomplishments.

The next year, at our annual convention, I spent time with Karen again. She shared with me that she was being squeezed out of her job by a younger woman. She asked me if I could help her find another position. As it happened, there was something available at my company. I recommended her highly, and she landed the job. We tried to solve the world's problems for women in our organizational work. Sometimes it comes down to helping one another, one-by-one. As Mother Teresa said, "Never worry about numbers. Help one person at a time. And always start with the person nearest you." After all that Karen had given to me professionally, I was gratified to be able to do something for her. That wonderful circle is how it should work.

Chapter Seven

Overcoming Perfectionism

"Perfection is a twenty ton shield that we lug around thinking it will protect us when, in fact, it's the thing that's really preventing us from taking flight."

—Brené Brown

"She is in a bad place. Please meet with her and give her a boost." That is what my dear friend Victoria said to me about her adult daughter, Jessica, during our monthly telephone conversation. I met my friend in journalism graduate school at Columbia University years ago, and we both went on to become journalists at newspapers located across the country from one another. Now we were both retired from those jobs. Victoria became involved in politics, and I was writing novels that had been writing themselves in my head for years. Jessica lived in the same city as I did, and we would sometimes get together when Victoria visited.

Jessica had followed in our footsteps by obtaining her graduate degree in journalism at Columbia. After graduation she married another writer, and had a daughter. She decided, at the age of twenty-six, that she would write a novel as her full time job, and she did. We were so proud of Jessica for her courage and discipline. She embellished upon experiences she had doing service work in the Dominican Republic when she was a teenager, and turned it into a murder mystery. It was truly a "page turner."

To her surprise, after much persistence and some heartache, she was able to get a literary agent, and then a respected publisher. The publisher gave Jessica a generous advance even though it was her first book. It ended up becoming a bestseller, and she won a prestigious award for a first time novelist. It was translated into many languages and marketed in the United States and abroad. Jessica gave book talks all around the country, and was asked to speak internationally. She appeared on major networks, and Netflix made a series of her book. She was well known on social media, with an abundance of followers.

Meanwhile, despite the early accomplishments in one area of her life, her marriage suffered and ended in divorce. Her husband was struggling as a freelance journalist, and had a difficult time coping with Jessica's career's meteoric rise. In addition, he resented having so much of the childcare responsibility when Jessica travelled, and he felt that it was interfering with his career success. He had an affair with a single woman neighbor on a different floor of their apartment house and moved out of their apartment and into the woman's apartment. The neighbor was a successful real estate broker with her own business, and she largely supported Jessica's husband while he tried to write his own novel.

All of this turmoil occurred fifteen years ago. Her ex-husband never finished his novel and never married the neighbor girlfriend. After two years with her, he moved to a different area of the country where it was less expensive to live, and did freelance writing. Jessica's ex-husband visited their daughter about three times a year, and spent time on the telephone and on FaceTime with her. He provided little financial support for their child. He wanted to be free of responsibilities, and he largely was.

Thus, during the early years of her daughter's life, Jessica was the primary caretaker and the breadwinner. She was able to afford to hire a nanny to help. With the money she earned from her successful debut novel and the series, she could also afford to attend graduate school to earn a degree in library science. She wanted financial security for herself and for her daughter. She thought that library work, while not high paying, would give her regular income, a pension, medical insurance, and a schedule which would provide her with a structure within which to incorporate her writing. She wanted a job where she would interact with people for her mental health. She wanted to be surrounded by books and learning, and she did not want the hard deadlines of journalism. She earned her degree, and took a position at a college library. Her life was quiet and steady, but somehow not completely fulfilling.

Even though the turmoil of the earlier years had lessened, and her daughter was getting ready to go to college, Jessica had not written any novels after her first. She had not written anything at all, except papers for her graduate program years before. She was suffering from this. Victoria thought that since I was able to write books without too much blocking me, that perhaps Jessica would benefit from talking to me about her frustration in not being able to write anymore.

I met Jessica near her library job at a local cafe. We had warm feelings for one another, and I knew that she looked upon me as though I were a treasured Aunt. We both knew why we were meeting. After exchanging a few pleasantries, I asked her to tell me what was troubling her. She said:

"I am struggling right now. Mom and I thought telling you about it might help me. I really appreciate your time. Unlike you, I am stuck, blocked, broken. The thing that I most want to do, write, is the one thing I can no longer accomplish. I am going for therapy about it, but I thought that sharing my thoughts with another writer might provide another avenue for healing. You have always provided a safe haven for even my most tortured thoughts.

My therapist believes that I have the classic signs of a perfectionist. I have always been hypercritical of myself. He believes that my striving to have standards of flawless, high performance; my critically evaluating myself; and my concerns with others' evaluations of me are causing my low self-esteem and depression. He did not tell me all of this directly. That is what I have gleaned from our sessions together.

Every time I sat down to start writing, my fear of failure took over and I procrastinated. At first I used the excuse that I was in graduate school and a single mother. Then I told myself that I was working full time and a single mother. Those were legitimate excuses. I was continually exhausted. But perhaps I could have scheduled writing sessions with all the other tasks. Then, when my daughter grew up and was busy with her own activities, I ran out of reasons for not writing.

I have been trying to figure out what is stopping me. One obvious reason is that I became addicted to the love and admiration I felt after my first novel, and grew afraid that I would be unable to continue to please my audience. Since I was lauded for my first novel, I was fearful that my next novel would not be successful and readers would think I am a fraud, an imposter. I already think that about myself. People sometimes cruelly enjoy bringing down a winner. I could picture them saying that I was one of those authors who was capable of one novel in her life-time, and that was it. I have a few pages in my drawer for five different novels.

I keep focusing on the results and it has sucked all of the fun out of the creative process. I set myself up for perpetual failure.

After my first novel, there were some criticisms of it. Instead of focusing on the accolades it received, I read and reread every negative thing that was said about it. I felt undeserving of the positive comments. I ruminated over a few typos which no one caught in the first edition of my book. No matter what I did in promoting the book, it was never enough for me. I am my harshest critic.

I have been delving back into my past to recall when perfectionism first took over my life. I remembered how important it was for me to please my father. If I achieved good grades, or some other accomplishment during my school years, he paid attention to me and gave me love. If I failed at anything, I felt his disapproval, acutely. My therapist called it "success-focused parenting."

I was always down on myself, even then, thinking I had to work so much harder than everybody else did in order to succeed. I have always felt myself to be flawed. When I was a teenager, I suffered from headaches, which have continued into my adult life. I suppose I have made it my life's work to be perfect for my father, which continued even after he died. He died young. The need to be acceptable to others extended from my father to everyone else.

My father was a perfectionist. As an architect, his work had to be flawless. He carried that trait over into everything he did. He painted for recreation, but continually reworked his canvases or destroyed them, never thinking that they achieved the perfection he wanted. He never showed his work to anyone. I expect that I inherited this trait from him, or perhaps he created that kind of environment in our home.

During my school years I wrote for the school newspaper. I remember I ripped up many articles. I felt that they were not good enough. I rewrote and edited my work so many times, I had difficulty meeting deadlines. I over-edited other people's work, and I annoyed other students I worked with because of my perfectionism. After journalism graduate school, I did not want to work at a job where I had constant deadlines, as I recognized that my perfectionism would make my work life painful for me.

I discussed my eating disorder with my therapist. He believed that my perfectionism correlated with that disorder. I remember that my father would criticize me if I gained weight, and he told me that boys and men would not be attracted to me if I was overweight. He also said that I would have more professional success if I remained thin. I remember if I ate something I was not supposed to, I felt terrible guilt and shame. That has continued. No matter how thin I am, I never feel thin enough. The need to be accepted and cared for are at the bottom of all of my perfectionism.

Social media is not helping me with my perfectionism. I look at other author's pages, and I make unhealthy comparisons between them and me. I am never satisfied with what I achieved, even though I successfully raised a daughter on my own, have two graduate degrees, a best selling novel, and a career as a librarian. I put myself down for being a librarian in that my father, likely, would have felt that it was somehow a lesser profession. My self-worth is tied up with my achievements, and how others perceive my achievements.

My relationships with men have been impacted in that I have been unable to sustain a long-term relationship. I am critical of myself and of them. I have been accused by my boy-friends of making them feel that they are never good enough, and no matter what they do, it fell short. I know that this trait has made it impossible for me to re-marry or to find a permanent partner. I have convinced myself that being in a relationship would prevent me from writing more novels, which is another excuse, I imagine, for not wanting to commit.

What is saddest for me is that I think my perfectionism has impacted negatively upon both my productivity and my creativity. I am afraid to start a new project and to make mistakes. My ideas are stale in my view. My personal standards are unreasonably high and unattainable. I avoid challenges, which makes it that much harder to achieve my own lofty goals. I have worked well in the structured environment of a college library where there were explicit instructions and goals to meet, and I have brought some creativity to that environment, but the creative world of writing eludes me.

I have felt so much pressure to live up to my previous achievements. I desire greatness but I fear that I could fail at the very thing that I desire greatly. I guess I am a paralyzed perfectionist. I am trapped into living a less meaningful life by my self-handicapping. I have discussed with my therapist that my perfectionism is used to protect me from blame, shame or judgment.

I was thinking about the lengths that I go to procrastinate when I should be sitting down to write. It takes me forever to actually sit down. I watch the news, linger over my coffee reading an article which could wait, fixate on chores around the house, send a slew of emails, and reorganize papers that do not need it. Then, once I finally sit down, I do not stay there for long. I make too many cups of tea. I check my cellphone often which completely interrupts my flow. I check out different sites on my computer, convincing myself that it is research for a future book. I begin to order items on Amazon which I do not need. How much do I write in a session? Maybe a paragraph. And then I delete it the next time I sit down."

I told Jessica some of my reactions to her comments after giving her a huge hug. She was so sincere, and I could feel her intense need to bring her creations out into the world again, coupled with the enormous pain she felt in trying to do so. She was working hard to change, and it was not going easily for her.

"I truly understand what you are facing. Many creative people struggle with your issues, but knowing you are not alone is not a complete cure. Perhaps by telling you about my writing journey, you will take some comfort, and it may generate a few ideas.

For forty-five years, as a journalist, I worked on deadlines. It was often difficult. I procrastinated constantly. I waited, routinely, until the last minute to send in my articles. I needed to have my adrenaline pumping in order to produce. It was only by operating with little time that I could convince myself that if I had more time the work would have been better. That way, in my own mind, I did not have to blame any imperfections on my skills or abilities.

My perfectionism had to take a back seat, to an extent, because the work had to go out or I would not get paid. I had to deal with critical editors, and some infighting and backstabbing in the office, but I managed to hold on. I was a workaholic to mask my insecurities about not measuring up. Sometimes my self-esteem suffered when I had particularly critical editors. A few editors who were themselves impossible imperfectionists, made me want to quit, but I outlasted them.

I put my own desire to write novels on hold as I was never proficient at multitasking. I could not succeed at my job, and write on the side, the way that others did. With all the writing I did for work, I wanted my free time to be engaged in other kinds of activities using other parts of my brain. I felt badly about myself that I could not create a novel all those years, but I was realistic about my own limitations, or, perhaps I self-sabatoged.

While I was working for others, I was stressed out all of the time because of my perfectionism. I had to work harder than everyone at the office. I had to write the most articles. I had to go home and make the perfect dinner. I had to have a spotless and well-curated home. I had to make certain that my children achieved high grades and participated in extracurricular activities and volunteer work. I had to groom myself to perfection so that my husband would continue to think I was attractive. I overreacted to every mistake and misstep, of mine and other family members. It was exhausting, and I was often angry, hostile and discontented because of it. I became easily depressed. I held myself and everyone else to such high standards that I turned my family and others off. I even found myself tiresome to be with at times.

One of the benefits of being an older, retired person, for me, is that I write for myself because the process, while sometimes painful, gives me joy and a sense of accomplishment. I want other people to connect with my work and to like it, but I am no longer burdened by my own unrealistic standards. I have silenced my critical inner voice. My work does not have to be perfect. It can be good enough.

I never achieved your level of success, so I cannot fully appreciate the benefits or burdens of that. There is nothing that can go wrong in my writing world. If no one wants to publish it, I have the option of self publishing. If I do not care about publishing, I can let my children, grandchildren and friends read my writing. If I want to keep my writing in a drawer for my eyes only, while I am alive, there is no judgment in that. I do not have to give up my writing for any reason. I do not have to procrastinate. My timetable is my own.

With all of this freedom came an interesting benefit. I am more productive than ever. I have no problem sitting and writing or editing for hours at a time. If I have an off day I research for the next part of the book. I work on only one book at a time which keeps me focused. I do not feel performance anxiety, and I do not feel disappointment about what I wrote. I do not feel shame about who I am. I have developed self-compassion. I suppose the pressure is off because I no longer care what others think about my writing. I am not worried about making mistakes or being rejected. Other people seem to like me better now too as I am easier to be around. I do not think about the results, just about the doing. Every time I complete a novel, I feel this wonderful sense of giving birth. The novel may not be perfect, but she came from my body, soul and spirit, and so in that sense the work is unique.

I prioritized action over doing things perfectly. If I write for a few hours each day, I pat myself on the back. Usually I write much more, but I did not put that requirement on myself. It just flows. I have much less stress now. They say that perfectionists are awash with stress and that they die earlier. I have too much to say, and am not ready to go. I read that perfectionists marry their identity with their achievements. I am trying to divorce myself from that kind of thinking. If you focus on achievements, you become averse to making mistakes. I no longer want gold stars from others to define my self worth. I do not want to believe that I am only worth something when I am getting others' approval. I want my own unconditional love and acceptance. This is liberating for me. I think that it will be liberating for you too to adopt this mindset. Maybe you do not have to wait as long as I did to get it."

Jessica shared some thoughts about becoming an imperfectionist:

"Interestingly, you have talked about many of the issues I have worked on in my therapy sessions. The pressure should be off of me because I have a day job. I do not have to rely on my novel writing to support me and my daughter. That thought makes it harder on me rather than easier. It is not about the money for me. You are retired with a pension and social security, so you do not have to make money through your novel writing either. We are both in privileged circumstances. But in your situation, you have taken that freedom, and run with it. You are striving for excellence, and you are driven by your passions. You are acting. You are unburdened by the expectations of others.

Some days I wish I had never written that first novel so early in my career. I sometimes think that if I had not achieved so much early success, I would not be paralyzed by it. I could have built my way up, instead of always worrying about toppling from the heights. But then I think about artists with early success who kept on producing and adapting with the times. Those comparisons are not helpful to me.

The better question is, how do I make the most of my circumstances now? How do I make my desire to write stronger than my fear? How do I internalize my successes? In addition to my therapy sessions, I have been doing a lot of reading about imperfectionism. Many of the writings talk about what you are saying, which is to focus on the process, and to take one step at a time. I am trying to take monthly steps for my novel writing.

How do you get yourself to think less about the results? How do you get to the point where you no longer care about being rejected, being judged, making mistakes and making everything perfect? We are social beings. Don't we all need the approval of others? Maybe the benefit of getting older is seeing that you really do not need that. For every person who does not support you or your work, there is another person who does, but in the end we have to love and approve of ourselves. That means getting other people out of your head. We can accept healthy criticism, but in the end, we have to decide which criticisms make sense for our own work.

We are counselled to give ourselves healthy self-talk, and that by thinking positively, results will improve. I am trying to power through my mistakes and to not set up rigid rules for myself. I am trying to care less and to focus on my effort over perfection. I was never a rebel, but healthy rebellions can be liberating. I have been doing things to loosen myself up. I meditate and do yoga. I draw with my non-dominant hand. I dress for my own comfort and pleasure. I try to spend time with people who have totally different mind-sets. I watch different news programs with opposing biases. I travel more. I eat foods from different cultures. I do all these things in an effort to convince myself that there is no one right way of living or thinking."

I told Jessica that her desire to change herself, her taking steps to free herself and to relax, her seeking the help of a well qualified therapist, her reading about perfectionism and imperfectionism, and her speaking with me and others, would all take time to marinate, but would result in her bringing herself to a different place. She was taking action on many levels. I said:

"In listening to you, I am convinced that you will write again. You are disciplined, and you care. Your caring too much, and about things which do not serve you well, have impeded your progress. Now that you have identified the origins of your perfectionism, how it has played out in your personal life and career, and how it has negatively impacted you in all of its manifestations, you are ready for the growth part.

After I retired, I began to think about why I wanted to write novels. As a somewhat introverted person, I wondered why I would want to expose myself to the public. Artists put themselves in a vulnerable place by opening up their minds and hearts. Many of us are sensitive. I thought about how writing had served me in the past. When I was younger, I found that writing for student literary journals and newspapers was a great outlet. I lived in my head alot, and wanted to share my thoughts with others. I preferred writing to speaking. Writing gave me time to gather my thoughts to express myself most truly. It gave me great pleasure to see my thoughts turn into words on a page. Sometimes I felt that I had nothing to do with their creation. The words came out of me in a spontaneous, unhampered way.

When I chose to make writing my profession by getting my graduate degree in journalism, and then working for newspapers as a reporter, I took pleasure in the hunt for information, and turning it into a newsworthy article. My goal was to inform the public. The constant strain of deadlines did take some of the enjoyment out of it, but overall, it was a good fit.

Now that I am writing about subjects I choose, the spontaneity is returning. The process is what interests me. I dream about my ideas for novels. I wake up in the middle of the night with ideas and write them down in my head. I walk every day after I do my writing. While I am walking, I work out problems with the writing in my thoughts. Wherever I am, whomever I am talking to, whatever I am observing and reading are all sources of inspiration for me. I love the sound of my clicks on the keyboard, and the words appearing on my computer screen. The editing and reorganizing of paragraphs gives me a sense of mastery. It gives me pleasure when I check my word count, and see how productive I have been, but I do not chide myself when the words do not flow. I know they will come another day. The sense of creation is so fulfilling.

I remember the adage that not everyone is going to like you no matter what you do. Not everyone is going to like your work either. I showed one of my novels to four different people. They all had different comments and none of their criticisms intersected. Their views were important, but in the end, I had to have the confidence to incorporate the comments which resonated with me and my vision.

From what you have told me, you do not have a problem generating ideas, but you get stuck when you try to write. Perhaps telling yourself while you write that you will not show your writing to the public will free you. Then, later, as you develop more confidence in yourself, you will share it. Maybe you will choose to share it with your mother, your daughter, or trusted and kind writer friends. Be careful who you pick. Your inner critic is still too harsh. You do not want a harsh outer critic.

What I have found is that the more I write, the more I want to write. We both have years and years when we did not write the type of writing we want to do now. All of those observations and stories are in us, waiting to be released. Our enjoyment of the process is reason enough. With regard to others, at the very least, if we show our work to supportive family members, we know that they will understand us better and how we think. It may provide them with insights and comfort. That connection alone is worth it. How much we want to disseminate the writings is up to us, but that is not the reason we write. We write because we have to. And when we do not, we get sick."

Jessica began to cry. She said:

"Yes, I feel sick now because utilizing my creative outlet, writing, is breathing to me, and I cannot write, therefore

I cannot breathe. That is reason enough for me to sit down every day to write, or as often as I can. Another reason I experience guilt and shame is that I am setting a bad example for my daughter. I try to give her confidence and courage to tackle her inner demons and to do what she has passion for. Words are empty if she does not see me living those words. I will try to use that to inspire me to write as my relationship with my daughter means so much to me."

I told Jessica that she should use anything to motivate her to write, but, in the end, she is doing it for herself. She needs to make her creative outlet a priority in her life, whether others benefit from it or not. Her writing is not about seeking approval, reducing her guilt or any other baggage. Her writing is about expressing herself. I told her that she needs to be selfish about her art. In that context, selfishness is good. It is about her health. It is about her well-being. She will be more present and inspirational to others if she is free to create. I said:

"People will attack you about your art. Now there is instantaneous criticism on social media. That is why you cannot pay attention to any of it. There will be those who will attack you because they cannot create due to their own blockages. There will be those who are jealous. There will be those who genuinely do not like your work. There are any number of reasons for you to get negative feedback about your writing. Nothing should stop you from creating. Why? Because you need it to breathe."

We wished each other health and productivity, and vowed to keep in touch and to meet again. Our schedules were busy. Two years later I met Jessica for coffee to catch up and to support one another's artistry. She had written two novels. One was scheduled for publication, and the other was in the editing and revision stage. She had found a new literary agent who supported her work, and a new publisher. She said that she had enjoyed the process of writing, and felt steadier and more sure of herself. She expressed concern about the marketing and sales, but she knew that no matter how successful the books would be in the eyes of the publishing industry, she was no longer under water struggling to breathe. She had her "sea legs" back. We rejoiced that she had an imperfect life.

Chapter Eight

When Your Dog Becomes a Person

"*Outside of a dog, a book is man's best friend. Inside of a dog, it's too dark to read.*"

—Groucho Marx

We shared a secret and we confessed it to one another. Alice was my neighbor in the apartment building we lived in. We shared many of the same sentiments. Approximately one-third of the residents of our apartment house owned dogs of all shapes, sizes, breeds and mixed breeds and were predominantly small because of the size of the apartments. Neither of us owned a dog. We did not want to go into elevators where there were dogs as we feared that if the elevator stopped working, we would be trapped in an enclosed space with an animal. Neither of us wanted our neighbors' dogs to sniff us, ever.

We resided in a neighborhood in an urban center where many of the residents in other buildings were also dog owners. Some of the dogs sported shoes, nicer outfits than we had, and elaborate haircuts. Some of their leashes were decorated with rhinestones. On occasion, the sidewalk looked like a doggie red carpet. Every day you could overhear a pet owner speaking to her dog as if it was another person. Some of the owners transported their pets in baby carriages outfitted with blankets and toys. People with dogs stopped other people with dogs to exchange pleasantries. Sometimes people without animals would stop other people walking dogs to admire and pet their charges. The sidewalks were littered with dog walkers walking three or four dogs at a time, all barking.

Not all of the owners picked up their pet's poop on the sidewalks, although many were diligent about it. That was when it was a brown carpet. You may have already gleaned our secret. Neither of us liked dogs, and, not surprisingly, there was some shame attached to it, on our part, perhaps because of the societal stigma of harboring such views.

We were not the kind of people that dog lovers would imagine us to be in order to dislike their pets. We were each married and had raised empathetic, high-functioning children who lived independently. We were humanitarians. We traveled the world and understood our connections with others in the world community. Alice had served in the Peace Corps when she was younger, in a remote village in Africa. We were concerned about the global environment and enjoyed nature. We recycled religiously. We were concerned citizens. We voted at every election, paid our taxes, held responsible jobs, volunteered in our community, and served on boards. I was a vegan, and Alice, while she refused to eat red meat, still wore her twenty-year- old fur coat when it became extremely cold because there was no other garment which kept her as warm.

It is true that probably the last choice for either of us would be to save for and go on a safari in our retired years. We did not like the thought of people hunting animals which would become extinct, on principle, although we would not spend our time fighting for animal rights as we thought that people's rights were more important. And yet, neither of us would dream of even killing an insect. Our breed was and is difficult to categorize.

We were not haters of dogs. We just did not like them and did not understand the need to have one as a pet, nor did we truly appreciate how they could become as loved as other members of the family, or revered even more than other humans in some instances. We were both afraid that dog lovers would not like us for our opinions, and therefore we mostly were not 'out of the closet' about it. As we were getting older, we had less and less we wanted to hide. Was it time to be real about it? Didn't we have a right to our views? If animal lovers could be compassionate toward animals, couldn't they seek to understand us?

One day I saw Alice at the elevator in the lobby of our building, and we agreed to go for a walk in the park over the next weekend, but not near the dog park, obviously. While we were in the lobby, several dogs bounded over to us, sniffed our private parts and shoes, and started barking. Neither of us was pleased, although we feigned good humor out of politeness and civility. Their owners looked so proud of their dogs, and seemed to derive so much pleasure from them, that we did not want to appear as spoilers.

During our walk, we decided to dissect the origin of our antipathy toward dogs, and how we felt about it up to the present. Alice shared that there were a few decisive events which shaped her views. She said:

"I grew up in a suburban neighborhood. A family, including their two young children, with whom we were close, lived across the street from our house with their large German Shepherd dog named Lazlo. Lazlo had behavioral issues which the owners tried to address by sending him to obedience school. Despite their best efforts, Lazlo remained wild. A small boy from the neighborhood approached him one day, and before anyone could stop him, Lazlo bit his face. The story was unclear as to whether the boy did anything to provoke it. The bite resulted in the boy needing rabies shots and an abundance of stitches. He sustained a large, permanent scar on most of one side of his face, and there were lasting bad feelings between their families.

After that Lazlo was chained up in the yard, and he howled constantly for all to hear. Needless to say, I was terrified of Lazlo for years.

Another friend on an adjacent street had a Miniature Collie. Her family treated their dog like a member of the family. I remember feeling their love for their pet, but not entirely understanding it. Their dog went out into their backyard all of the time, and ran around and around a particular tree ceaselessly, until they called her to come inside. Their family thought that her circling around the tree was so amusing. It looked stupid to me and I did not understand their fascination with it. To them, it was similar to watching their babies doing adorable things, and oohing and aahing.

During college the dogs ran free on the quad. Some sported red bandanas. They largely left me alone and I ignored them. One of my roommates had a boyfriend who spent a lot of time at our house in Collegetown. He always stayed over with his dog, but we were concerned because his dog was untrained, and he beat the dog and yelled at him constantly. The dog was constantly running away. Like some domestic violence victims, the dog would return to his abuser for food and treats, which alternated with hits and threats, and kept the dog in a forever loop of running away and coming back for more of both.

We were afraid that the dog would turn on us with displaced rage. We were more worried that, in addition to the animal cruelty to his pet, the boyfriend would beat our friend when she did not do what he wanted her to. We heard him yelling at her too. When their relationship ended, none of us were unhappy. We remained concerned about what he would do to the dog and other women. We never found out.

Years passed, and I did not think much about dogs until I heard about what happened to one of my closest friends. She was and is one of the gentlest people I have ever known. Since our graduate school days, she and her husband have always owned large dogs. On one occasion, she was 'babysitting' for a neighbor's dog, and went into their yard to feed it. The dog attacked her, bit her on her face and other places, and she had to have multiple stitches, and then plastic surgery. I never understood why she remained a dog lover. For me, however, that was further proof that animals can be dangerous and unpredictable, and therefore unsuitable as domestic pets.

When my friend moved cross country with her dog, her animal was having a terrible time adjusting to their new home and could not be left alone. The dog barked and whimpered continually, and for hours, whenever my friend left the house. It became so painful for my friend, she stopped leaving her house for a time, which impeded her ability to find a job and new friends. She took the dog for therapy. It took a long time for the dog to improve. My initial reaction was that she should find a place for the dog where there were other animals for company, and people who were home more than her life would permit. I tried not to share that view too strongly, as I was afraid I might lose a friend over my opinions since I clearly did not 'get it.' I could not understand shaping your schedule around a pet as if it was a baby or child. Does that make me selfish?

Recently, and about a decade after she had been bitten on her face, I saw the same friend for a mini-reunion. She and her entire family had remained dog lovers, and they all liked large dogs. My friend and her husband had a dog, and both of her adult daughters, who lived in their own places, each had dogs. Her daughters, like her, were petite, and looked as if they weighed not much more than their pets. They posted pictures on facebook with their pets.

I observed that my friend had brown crusted scabbed skin all over the outer portion of one of her hands. She told me that she had been taking care of one of her daughter's dogs while her daughter was on vacation. While she was walking it, the dog tried to eat some food, which was garbage on the ground, and she pulled the dog back sharply with the leash. The dog resisted violently. The leash cut into her hand and burned right through the skin. She still loves all dogs, including her daughter's dog. How can that be?"

I replied to Alice, "good question." I shared with Alice that I had a frightening incident involving a dog when I was an adult.

"We went to a good friend's weekend home overnight. They had two large dogs, one of which was being treated with prozac and had behavioral issues. They thought that perhaps that dog had been mistreated before they adopted him. That dog tended to bite, and nipped me hard several times on my behind. That dog also bit the owner's sister on a prior occasion. Neither her sister nor I wanted to be in the presence of the dog anymore. To my friend's credit, the dog was either locked in a different room, or not present at all when people who feared him visited subsequently, at great expense for them in that they had to hire a doggie babysitter.

They never considered returning the dog to the shelter, or finding another home for it. They kept that dog until it died, with all of its problems. After that experience, my antipathy toward dogs increased even more. My friend's husband once told me that he did not trust people who did not like dogs. I understood where he was coming from, but my thought, which was equally judgmental, was how could owners keep a dog that had bitten more than one person."

Alice mentioned that she had other, perhaps more trivial objections to having a dog. "We were not pet people in my family when I was growing up. We decided that they were too expensive for our household budget, and none of us pushed to have one. In addition to being afraid of them, I personally find dogs to be smelly and dirty. I hate seeing their excrement on sidewalks and streets where I take my walks. The worst is to step on it unwittingly, to bring it into your apartment, and to be unable to easily clean it off of the bottom of your shoes. It is completely unacceptable to me when I see a dog eating throw up off the floor, or anything else they happen to find on the ground.

I find dogs annoying the way that they always seek attention, which interferes with my sense of order and with my need for peace and quiet. Dog owners expect me to express admiration for their dogs, and to touch their animals. I find it repulsive to touch their dirty fur, to be drooled on, to be licked, to have a dog sniff me all over, including my private parts, and to have a dog wrap its legs around one of my legs and start to hump me. I do not want to have dog hair on my clothes and shoes, nor do I want my shoes to be destroyed by their chewing.

People who have dogs have smelly apartments, houses and cars with drool, pee and hair on their furniture and floors. I do not look forward to spending time in those environments. I had one relative we visited regularly as a family when I was a child. She had a dog and a cat. I remember feeling repulsed by the state of her apartment, which inevitably had dog poop or urine on the floor, and furniture which had been destroyed and pulled apart at the seams.

Unfortunately for me, dog lovers do not limit their dog's activities to their homes, yards or apartments, or to bringing their animals to parks. They carry and walk their dogs on planes, trains and buses, and to supermarkets, restaurants, movies, concerts and other gatherings. They expect others to appreciate their pets. I find it intrusive to not have the choice once a pet enters my space. On a busy city sidewalk, being near dogs can be treacherous as one gets tangled in the leashes, or one trips trying to avoid stepping on them. And when several dogs with separate owners find themselves in a small space on the sidewalk, as they bark and attack one another, it feels Darwinian. Any sense of calm I may have had disappears.

I have the opinion, also, that keeping dogs in a small city apartment is cruel to the animals. Keeping them as pets, instead of letting them run free on a farm or in the country, does not serve them well, in my view, although their human owners enjoy it. Aren't dog owners being selfish? City dog lovers make me feel unloving for having those sentiments, but we should be able to have a diversity of views and accept that we are all different, as to this topic, and others. I never get that kind of feedback from animal people. They consider me a breed apart, as I do them, I suppose."

I told Alice that I shared her opinions, but I emphasized that we are in the minority it would seem. I said:

"There are conflicting statistics about how many pet owners there are in the United States, but I have seen studies which indicated that sixty-two percent of the population lives with pets. We know that Americans have a great love for pets as evidenced by the amount of and price of pet foods in stores, the proliferation of videos, and the number of dog parks, dog walkers, grooming parlors, and emotional support animals. Some literature provides that there are people who seem predisposed to having pets, and that the pet-keeping habit often runs in families. It is clear that pets play an important part in many people's lives.

Since we see so many more dogs than other pets on the streets where we live, I want to talk with you solely about dog owners. I feel safe talking to you about it, as I know you will not judge me. There are many things that I cannot understand about people who love dogs. I cannot fathom why people treat their dogs like humans. It is incomprehensible to me that they would be considered part of the family. It is puzzling to me that people would want to constantly post pictures of their dogs on social media.

One friend, who was trying to convince me to become a dog lover, argued that loving a dog does not take away from all humans, including children, and that, in fact, dogs help children to develop improved self-esteem, motor skills, and better performance in school. She argued that there should be no limit to love in the world, to kindness and to positivity, and that dogs are living, breathing and feeling creatures worthy of a lifetime of love and care. It is hard to argue with that notion without feeling guilty.

Another pro-dog argument may be the health question. The results of studies have been mixed. Some of the literature states that having a dog can benefit the pet owner's physical and mental health. There are claims, especially with urbanite pet owners, that having a dog can reduce the risk of heart disease, provide improved immune response and increased physical activity, combat loneliness, and alleviate depression. Other studies maintain that having a pet has no, or if anything, only a slight negative impact on health. The negative effects include dog bites, the spreading of disease, asthma and other allergies, and associations with a higher incidence of heart attacks.

Other research concludes that with respect to health, any differences between pet owners and non-pet owners are not due to the fact of owning a pet, but rather factors like income, education, employment, housing, age, gender, race, and marital status. Apparently it is the demographics and lifestyle which are different. For instance, pet keeping is more common among white homeowners who have a higher household income. Because there is a strong inverse relationship between social class and health, that factor accounts for health differences, not necessarily pet ownership.

The fact of the matter is that even if I knew with scientific accuracy that a dog would improve my health I would not want one. How could I say that when dogs can be your best friend, fill an emotional void, and give you genuine unconditional love? Why wouldn't I want a companion who was loyal, obedient and kind? What about the dogs who help people with medical impairments?"

Alice listened to me, and said she felt that her own feelings were validated in that she shared my sentiments. She replied:

"We should not feel guilty for our dislike of dogs based upon our backgrounds, our personal experiences and our feelings. Even if we do not want to own one, we can still appreciate the functions that dogs perform in our society, for instance, the comfort dogs, the search and rescue dogs, the bomb-detecting TSA dogs, and the canine ambassadors. There are dogs which serve as part of military units, at border crossings, in airports, and at urban police departments. There are dogs which travel with humans into natural disasters, accidents, crime scenes and terrorist strikes and provide relief and comfort. Dogs are permitted as support animals on certain college campus dorms to help cope with the stresses of higher education. There are dogs used to calm children at dental offices. There are even dogs going onto surf boards with disabled people to raise money for the disabled.

What do dog lovers admire about their dogs? I spoke with some of my dog-loving friends. One said that their dog has a calming effect on the family, a playful and silly side which provides fun for all, and that their dog gives them unconditional love. He claimed that their dog has heightened intuition and seemed to sense who needs him the most and will gravitate toward that person. He claimed that dogs have interspecies social intelligence, can intuit what humans and other animals are thinking, and can be empathic.

Another dog lover said she appreciates the companionship her dog provides, the fact that the dog provides a guarding, protective function, and she enjoys the soft, warm feel of a dog against her skin. She sleeps with her dog every night, provides extra space on the couch for the dog, and has birthday celebrations for it. One friend, who goes to a cabin in the country regularly, said that he uses his dog to hunt, and that when he was growing up on a farm, they had dogs who worked with them to herd other animals and that they were wonderful workers. One friend said she is allowed to bring her dog to work, and works better with him there."

I told Alice that all of these good things people say about their dogs makes me feel a little unloving for having the views I have. I went on:

"Some people love their dogs in a measured way, but not comparable to what they feel for their family or friends. I can relate to that to an extent. Other people seem to want to engage with their dogs on an emotional, spiritual and intellectual plane which to me seems a bit extreme. There is a part of me that believes that people who love their dogs as if they were people, and in some instances more than other humans, are somehow misguided. Perhaps that is an unfair judgment. Despite my opinion, more and more people are viewing their dogs as valued members of their families. I read about pet health insurance becoming widely available. I learned about elaborate end-of-life rituals, including funerals and cremation urns, for dogs who die, and grief support sessions for the owners of deceased pets.

I am aware that almost one-third of Americans feel that animals should have the same rights as people, which include the right to be cared for and fed, the right not to be tortured, and the right to be with their families. They argue that dogs are intelligent and sentient and are capable of suffering, and that in our ability to suffer and our desire to live and be free, we are all equals.

Somehow I am not convinced that pets should be lavished with the same love, attention and resources as our children. Popular culture, with dogs portrayed in the media as having human qualities, brainwashed us that pets are like humans. I know that children and animals are considered innocents and helpless, and we have an innate desire to protect and nurture them because of that quality, or so I have read.

Perhaps the strongest reason people sometimes love their dogs equally or more than humans is that dogs provide their owners with unconditional love, which they cannot get anywhere else, at least not easily. Unconditional love has been defined as love without conditions, or affection without limitations. Should all love be considered equal no matter the source? Some argue that our love and care for animals frees us to be fully human."

As Alice and I were walking home, we observed a doggie park with many dogs and owners all congregating together with smiles on their faces engaged in conversations. Along the street, we saw a doggie day care center filled with many dogs of different breeds in a room, through a large glass window that we could look into to observe them. We passed a pet store, and a pet grooming establishment. We observed an elderly woman pushing her dog in a stroller. Her outfit matched her dog's outfit. She was out of her apartment enjoying the sunshine.

Alice and I looked at each other and smiled. None of these sights really moved us, truth be told. We shared that we were never going to want to own a dog, that we would seek companionship and love elsewhere, and that we would save our need to nurture and protect for our children and grandchildren. We acknowledged that our talking with each other about all of our conflicting feelings helped us to feel human. It was human connection we both sought, and would continue to seek. We acknowledged that we would never totally understand dog lovers, nor would they understand us, but we hoped that everyone would feel free to have diverse views, without too much judgment on either side. We arrived at our elevator in our building. Alice said to me in parting, with a twinkle in her eye, "every dog must have his day, and so should every human."

Chapter Nine

On Being Selfish, Self-Absorbed, And Self-Centered

"Selfish persons are incapable of loving others, but they are not capable of loving themselves either."

—Erich Fromm

"I have been a selfish being all my life, in practice, though not in principle."

—Jane Austen

It was time for Rebecca. She was in her late thirties. She wanted to understand more about having healthy and good relationships with men. This was not knowledge easily acquired at the prestigious, high-priced educational institutions she had attended. There was a limit to what she could glean from reading self-help books or her online research. She craved human interaction to sort out the issue of relationships. Wasn't that the point of any real relationship–it happened face to face?

Truth be told, she was looking for a permanent commitment from a mate, but could not seem to find it. She kept choosing the wrong men who were, in her view, selfish, and eventually the relationships all ended. Rebecca attended individual therapy sessions with a woman named Aphrodite who was credentialed as a psychologist, marriage counselor and relationship coach.

They had been exploring the ways in which Rebecca's selfishness, too, might have contributed to her lack of success in coupling. Rebecca tried to discuss relationship issues with family and friends, but either they did not know what she should do, or they offered advice that, largely, she could not entirely relate to.

At Aphrodite's suggestion, Rebecca signed up for a workshop at the local community center for couples and individuals, which was taught by Aphrodite. It was about how to have healthy relationships. The program was designed to help strengthen relationships with spouses or partners. For those not in a committed relationship, it provided information about ways to choose a suitable partner.

One of the sessions of the class dealt with the issue of selfishness, and its implications for relationships. Aphrodite defined selfishness as being "concerned excessively or exclusively, for oneself or one's own advantage, pleasure, or welfare, regardless of others." Now Rebecca could hear and learn from what her classmates had to say about this issue too.

Aphrodite started off the session by differentiating selfishness from self-care, and by talking about selfishness versus mutual support. She told us:

"Self-care is important, and we all need to prioritize our psychological and physical health by having a healthy diet, exercising, getting good sleep, relaxing, and engaging in enjoyable activities. You cannot help others if you do not take proper care of yourself first. A corollary of this is that we have to self-love, which is to recognize and nurture your own needs and desires.

As we will discuss in this segment, selfishness is different from self-care and self-love for our purposes. The implications of selfishness have long been discussed in the contexts of religion, philosophy, psychology, economy and evolution, and there are divergent views about it.

Some say that in our society today, selfishness is acceptable, encouraged, and has now reached epidemic proportions. Everybody is searching for ways to get their needs met. We see other words used to describe selfishness such as self-absorbed, self-centered, self-indulgent and narcissistic. We read about the gimme generation which includes people who are more interested in enhancing their personal gratification, and leading double lives to achieve it, more than ever before. We are told that the 'me' versus 'we' orientation is destroying relationships.

We cannot escape from the fact that we live in a competitive, individualistic culture, but we can find many instances, also, where people cooperate and provide mutual aid. Humans are social animals, and we need support, affection and love in intimate relationships in order to thrive. Romantic partnership relationships, which is what we are talking about in this course, are, by definition, about concern not just for oneself but for others. Each of you needs to figure out what you need and want from your relationships, and partners need to provide mutual support by standing by one another in all of each other's endeavors unconditionally and without judgment. All of this is easier said than done, which is why you are all here.

I provided you with materials, which are also available online, about healthy relationships. It includes information on learning to love yourself, creating space for both people, communicating well, being honest with one another, providing loving criticism, being respectful of each other's opinions, forgiving and asking for forgiveness, and encouraging your partner. The goal is to make one another feel loved and appreciated. You need to provide one another with environments of mutual support in which you show caring for each other's emotional well-being, and this can be achieved by continually inquiring about each other's thoughts and feelings to show that you are concerned about one another.

You have to monitor your own emotional state in order to achieve this, and not react out of anger, fear or jealousy. The side benefits are that you gain insights from your partner's perspective which expands your worldview and you can provide each other with the confidence to pursue creative projects which you may not have otherwise done on your own. The end goal is to live with compassion, to forgive the mistakes of the other, and to experience joy in the little things and with each other.

For those of you who do not yet have a partner, these are important issues to think about. Creating and maintaining these relationships can be difficult, as we all know. We are told not to be selfish as children, but there are natural biological impulses and social pressures which result in our behaving selfishly. Eventually we all develop selfish psychological patterns which we must unlearn and replace with a selfless compassionate pattern.

Selfishness takes a toll on relationships. What happens when couples get in selfish standoffs? People have different needs and inevitably there will be a clash. Partners start to worry less about pleasing the other person over time. There has been a rise in infidelity and divorce, which is symptomatic of the selfishness epidemic. What does selfishness in a romantic relationship look like to each of you? Please go around the room and share your perceptions.

Introduce yourself by using your first name."

"My name is Mark. My relationship fell apart because of a standoff. I was a surgeon and needed to live close to the hospital in Manhattan. My wife wanted to live in Brooklyn. When we married and raised our family, I agreed to move to Brooklyn to make her happy, even though it was a commute of over one hour for me each way. It made my life much more difficult than it needed to be, but she had friends and family there, and so I recognized the value for her. She complained that I was not home enough, but if I had not had the commute, I would have had more time at home. She chose not to work outside of the home, but insisted upon a full-time cleaning person and a full-time nanny for the children. We led a privileged life. So what was the problem you might ask, if you think that material comforts solve all problems?

I asked very little of her, in my view. I needed her to attend certain professional functions with me as everyone else was bringing their spouse. She refused as she did not feel comfortable at these gatherings, and thought I was unfair to ask her. Because of the organizations I belonged to, doctors from around the world would visit New York. When I wanted to entertain them, she would often refuse to go out with us or to let me invite them over. My parents lived in California. She did not like them and refused to go with me when I visited them.

She insisted that I pay for her plastic surgeries, that I fund the constant redecoration of our brownstone, and that I give her unlimited access to use our joint credit card as she pleased. If I did not agree initially, she would manipulate me until she got what she wanted. It seemed that she preferred material acquisitions over me. I worked harder and harder to provide her with her requests. It was never enough.

The children grew up and moved out of our home. I was still performing surgeries. I told her that the commute was taking a toll on my health, and begged her to move into Manhattan. Sometimes I had to travel at night to perform the surgeries. She refused. I bought a small apartment in Manhattan for weekdays, and kept our brownstone in Brooklyn. She declined to stay in the apartment in Manhattan. As you might imagine, we eventually divorced. My feeling was that she lacked empathy for me, and destroyed our relationship by continually being selfish. It seemed as though she had no concept of mutuality. She would say I was being selfish with each of my requests. But she never gave in. On the other hand, she probably thinks that she always gave in."

"My name is Al. In my case, I imagine I was the selfish one. I was pampered by my mother as a child, and was used to having my own way. I grew up in a different era. After I married Rosanna, she said she wanted to live in the country, and I said I needed the energy of the City. We lived in the City. I promised her that someday I would move part-time to the country, if only on weekends. That day never came.

I did not help Rosanna much with the cooking, housework or with the children. My mother always did the housework, and raised us, so that is what I knew. I grilled food in the summer, at a local park, and that was about it. I worked all of the time on construction jobs, and we lived paycheck to paycheck. Some of the work was seasonal. She wanted to get a job outside the home to help out. I told her no. I kept us on a tight budget and did not treat her to many things. If I wanted a boys night out, I took it. I rarely gave her time to go out on her own. When extra cash came in, I bought myself an expensive car, or some equipment or tools. I did not ask her how we should spend the money.

Many times I forgot her birthday and our anniversary. I always expected her to make a big deal out of my birthday. I wanted to be number one in the household, and to have everything revolve around me. She did not complain. Her father treated her much worse when she was growing up. He was an alcoholic, and hit her and her mother.

One year Rosanna started to complain of various aches and pains. I ignored it, and told her it was in her head and that she needed to stop being so weak. Over time, although she stopped complaining, she was able to do less and less. Eventually, she did go to the doctor, not at my insistence, and learned that cancer had spread throughout her body. She died within a few months. I bought her a coffin, and the most inexpensive cemetery plot I could find in that I felt that I would need the money. My children accused me of being cheap with her in life and in death, and of being too selfish to realize their mother was so ill. They blamed me for her not living longer.

A short time after she died I started to date. I was not doing well living alone as I was not used to taking care of myself. My children lived in other cities. I was not having much luck finding relationships. The women I dated told me that my view of roles in a relationship was outdated. Finally, I met a woman who grew up the way I did. She wanted to be my housekeeper, cook, and to take care of me. I just needed to pay the rent. I did and do more for her than I did for my poor wife. You could say that I learned my lesson. I show her that I care more. I bring home flowers on occasion, buy her jewelry, treat her to dinners out, and take vacations with her. I listen to what she wants, and try to give it to her. I help more around the house. Am I still selfish? Probably. But the balance is better, at least from my new woman's point of view."

My name is Laurie. I hate to use labels, but for shorthand purposes, I was married to a narcissist. Afterwards, I kept dating narcissists. It seems that I am continually attracted to the same kind of man. They were all preoccupied with their own success and had a grand sense of their self-importance. All of them had a difficult time maintaining connections with other people, including with me. They had some common characteristics. They lacked empathy, they had manipulative tendencies, they felt entitled, and craved attention and admiration. I know that healthy selfishness requires self-love, which they did not have.

I will describe my relationship with Peter as an example of what I am talking about. Peter had a fragile sense of self. He needed to feel better than other people and did so by putting them down. He criticized me all of the time. For instance, he told me that he kept himself in great shape, and asked me why I did not work out more so that my body would be better. He bought me ten spin classes without asking me. Instead of being grateful, I resented it. I thought it was a covertly disguised put-down. He probably thought it was generous of him. I know it is important to look at the motivations behind the behavior to see if the seeming unselfishness is bad or good. He bragged about his academic credentials next to mine, too.

He lauded his own achievements and told me that I was lazy and lacked curiosity. He rarely, if ever, complimented me, and had little regard for my talents or abilities. He thought that his work as a corporate CEO was more important than my work as a social worker. He made fun of how little money I made, and bragged about how much money he earned. He wanted to feel superior physically, intellectually, and financially.

Peter would show me, in every way, that I was not as important as he was, and that he had no regard for my time or interests. He always showed up late, or he broke a plan last minute if something more important for him came up. His work was always more pressing than mine. He would ask me to miss important work meetings or events as a way of showing my love for him. If I did not, he would say I was being selfish.

I was definitely the 'giver' with Peter and with the others. My friends describe me as a compassionate person. All of those men seemed to be attracted to that trait, and knew how to manipulate me because of it. As a child, I was raised with the precept that it is better to give than to receive, and that the secret to happiness lies in helping others. Narcissists know how to take advantage of that.

Peter wanted to destroy the happiness in others so that he could deal with the unhappiness within himself. His needs were insatiable. I could never give him enough time or attention. He kept on taking and taking. He viewed me, and everyone else, from the standpoint of their usefulness to him. He could not self-love or love others.

Narcissists often lose out in the end, because emotional manipulation can have bad long-term consequences. They have to win and make you lose. Emotional manipulators make their partners do things they do not want to do by making the partner feel guilty if they do not, or by behaving in an unpleasant way, such as yelling or withdrawing until they get what they want at the other's expense. In a relationship, the partner, in my case me, may be less likely to cooperate voluntarily, and may leave, shun and avoid the selfish one. One-sided relationships are doomed to fail.

I left Peter. The decisive moment when I decided to do so was the night I was to receive an award for service by a not-for-profit group at a fundraising dinner for that organization. It was an important honor for me, and I had filled a table with my family and closest friends. Peter was supposed to attend as my companion. His ticket was expensive, and I had paid for it.

He was trying to raise money for a project, and a potential donor was unexpectedly scheduled to be in town that night. At the last moment, Peter cancelled attending my dinner, and went out with the donor for dinner and drinks. I knew at that moment that the fact that he prioritized his every-day work over a very significant moment in my life was a big 'red flag.' I needed to be self-loving and selfish in a positive way. I finally removed him from my life. I hope that I can learn how to do better when picking out potential mates."

"My name is Edward. My wife is here, Mary, and I know she has her own version of this story. We do not have children. The way in which I experience selfishness with Mary is with how she spends, or does not spend, our money. I imagine finances are one of the subjects many couples fight over, but our experience will probably sound like role reversal. Mary came from a poor family. They struggled over money the entire time she was growing up. She was extremely bright, won some scholarships, and took out student loans to finance her college and MBA degrees. For the past fifteen years, she has been earning high salaries and bonuses, and is a senior executive at an insurance company.

I work as a teacher in middle school. As you know, teachers earn low salaries, but we do have wonderful benefits, at least in our state, including health and disability coverage, vacation time, and a generous pension at the end of our careers. During the summers, I work at a camp to earn extra money. I grew up in a family of educators as both of my parents were teachers. We never had a great deal of money, but we never worried about it. We travelled extensively as a family, and attended many cultural events together. We went out to restaurants for a family dinner on Sunday night each week.

Mary is afraid to spend money. She paid off all of her loans a long time ago, so there is no rational reason for it. I will give you a few examples of how her thriftiness, and hence, selfishness, manifests itself. We live in a small, one bedroom apartment with no light in the back of the building. The air quality is poor, and we get mold on the walls. It is a walkup, and we are on the fourth floor. In the winter, the apartment is quite cold. She keeps the temperature exceedingly low to save money. It is uncomfortable. We could afford to get a better apartment, but Mary refuses. I believe it is selfish of her to decline to move to a more habitable apartment, especially since we can easily afford it.

To me, vacations are important, and as a teacher, I am given a generous amount of time off. Mary, as a senior executive, gets significant vacation time too. She never takes all of her vacation, and told me that she only wants to take two small vacations per year, usually to places in driving distance from our apartment. I want to travel the world, and so I often have to go alone. It seems selfish to me that she would not do so knowing that I have a strong desire for adventure.

I like to go out to restaurants, and to try different ethnic foods in diverse neighborhoods. Mary did not grow up going to restaurants, and she thinks that it is a frivolous use of our money since we can cook healthier foods at home. If I want to go out to a restaurant, I have to go alone or with a friend during lunch hour. When we go food shopping she brings coupons. I do not have a problem with that. But if something I want is not on sale, she argues with me that I should not get it, even if it is only a matter of a few dollars.

It seems to me that all of these differences, and more, which I will not go into, coupled with Mary's unwillingness to compromise, are selfish responses. Her version of pleasure is to deny herself, and, hence to deny me. So while she is not spending our joint income on things or experiences just for herself, she is not living a generous life, which deprives me."

"My name is Mary. All of what Edward says is true, but I do not consider myself selfish. I consider Edward selfish for continually asking to spend money on a lavish lifestyle, and then when I do not want to go along with it, to spend the money on those items anyway for himself on his own. I am the money manager in our family because of my financial background. I prepare our budget, pay the bills, and manage our investments. What Edward did not mention is that I would like to retire at an early age. I cannot do so if we spend a lot of money on an expensive apartment, vacations and restaurant dining.

In addition, Edward's parents are still alive while mine are not. Because his parents spent their money when they were younger, they are running out of money in their old age. We give them money each month to supplement their meager pensions and social security checks. The one way I admit to being selfish in my thoughts is that I wish that we did not have to do this. I have always had the discipline to have long-term goals, and to deprive myself of some of my 'wants' in the short-term. Thomas and his parents have different ideas about money, but they need someone like me to bail them out. I do not want to work forever depriving myself of my dreams, while fueling other people's."

"My name is Ann. We have different issues in my marriage. My husband John and I fight continually about 'who does what,' and about how to discipline our three children. He is here and can give his side of it. We each think that the other is selfish.

John expects me to do everything for our children since I work part-time from the home. I think that is selfish. Working part-time is like working full-time except without the pay and benefits. Also, working from home can be a nightmare with the children banging on my office door begging and crying to be let in during my working hours despite the fact that I hired a babysitter to entertain them for those periods. John has the luxury of going to his out-of-home office, interacting with others as an adult, and closing his office door when he needs quiet time to work.

When John arrives home from work, he does not jump in to help me right away. He tells me that he needs transition time. I need time to make dinner without having the children underfoot. I feel he is being selfish by not helping immediately. I do most of the housework, including all of the laundry. On the weekends, he could pitch in more, but he does not. He tells me that he needs to catch up on sleep, he sleeps late, and then when he does shopping errands, he takes off on long car rides, leaving me at home with the three children. While he does handle our checking account, he could balance it and do all the banking right from his cellphone. He could do that during his lunch hour.

As to the discipline of the children, since I spend the most time with them, I like to run a 'tight ship.' I have no problem saying 'no' to them, and requiring them to behave and not to whine to get what they want. Since John is not home as much, and works long hours, he gives in to their every want. If they want a specific toy, he will buy it for them. If they want to go out for ice cream, he will take them. If they want to have play-dates, he will let them invite their friends, and then expect me to supervise it exactly at the time I am hoping for down time. We each think that the other is selfish in our handling of life's chores, and in our dealings with the children."

"My name is John. It is true, I love to spoil my children. I have to work extremely long hours at a high pressure job. I work in a competitive environment, I have a difficult boss, and coworkers who are not supportive. We have enormous bills with a house and three children. We agreed that it would be better for the family for Mary to work part-time, but it puts a lot of financial pressure on me. Giving things to my children is my way of making up for whatever my schedule deprives them of. In some sense pleasing the children makes working worthwhile. I recognize that it makes Ann's job more difficult. I need to try harder with that.

When I arrive home at night, it is usually 7:00 p.m., or later. I can barely function. I have a two-hour commute each way. I feel that Ann is selfish in wanting to hand off the children to me the second I walk in the door. I do help around the house and with the children, much more than Ann said, but perhaps not exactly at the times and in the ways she wants. On weekends, I need a little extra time to sleep. I feel that Ann is being selfish in not understanding that. On weekdays, I put all three children to sleep and read them stories. It should not be too much to ask for a little leeway on the weekend mornings.

We both work too many hours; Mary with her part-time job and then taking care of the children until I get home, and me with my commute, long hours at the office, and sometimes work when I get home in the evening, including helping with the children. We do not have family in the area to assist us. We try to trade off with other families in the neighborhood to help one another, but sometimes it is more work than help. Perhaps neither of us is selfish. We just need to figure out how to please each other more in little ways which will make our schedules more tolerable."

"My name is Rebecca. Listening to those of you with children makes me realize some of the challenges ahead of me if I find a suitable mate and have children. There is a lot of effort involved in everything from finding someone, living together, starting and maintaining a family, and keeping the relationship alive through it all. How to get what you want and need, without being selfish, involves a lot of creativity it would seem, and constant calibration.

Many of my friends have settled down and have children. There are a few of us who have not been able to find someone. My friends told me that I am too picky. When they asked me what I am looking for, I profess to wanting someone who is handsome with a good body, athletic, intellectual, and has a well-paid career and is from a nice family. Perhaps what I should be focusing on are their qualities such as kindness, loyalty, honesty, generosity and stability.

I used many different dating apps. My friends told me that I am not choosing well, or that I wasted my time on certain men who found me. The guys knew that they are a swipe away from finding someone else, and at my age they seem to have more options. Since at my stage of life I do tend to focus on superficial traits, I go out with good-looking guys who perhaps have more prospects than the others. I have dated many guys who want me to dress a certain way, to wear a certain perfume, to lose or gain weight, and who were controlling in so many other ways. They tended to want things the way they wanted them, and had a certain arrogance. I seem to be attracted to arrogance, but then it wears thin.

The guys I dated all appeared to be selfish in their own ways. They seemed to have a firm belief in their absolute freedom of choice. They worked as much as they wanted to, but if I had to work they were not understanding. They wanted to choose the restaurants, the vacation places, the activities we did, the people we spent time with, and the food we cooked together.

The more compliant I was, the happier they were and the more unhappy I was. They wanted to text more than talk, so that there was the illusion of companionship without the demands of a relationship. They seemed to be disinterested in true partnership relationships or concepts of mutuality or reciprocity.

The men I dated often told me that I was selfish. They said that I put my work first. They said that I had too many strong opinions and wanted my own way. They said that I was demanding and controlling. I was called bossy more than once. I saw myself as a strong, independent woman who wanted a strong, independent man. They saw me as someone who was difficult to manage because I had my own point of view.

After listening to all of you, I know that I need to look at my own behavior, and find a compromise I can live with when I find someone to love. I have been told that my generation is more selfish than some other generations. We are accused of having higher rates of narcissism, materialism and technology addiction. We are told several other things about our generation such as 'that we are manipulated by advertising to be more materialistic; that we are searching for ourselves which is why we take so many selfies; that we are exposed to social media which makes us sadder; that we have more workplace stress and job insecurity, which makes us selfish; that we are exposed to the rise of celebrity culture which perverts our values; and that we have a pervasive sense of disquiet which leads to narcissism in our relationships.'

I do not know if all of that is true, but I do know that men and women are confused about their roles and what works. We have memories about how our parents and other adults functioned in their relationships. We have new thoughts about the roles of women and men. My job is just as prestigious as the men I date, even though I get paid less for the same work.

Although I work in a typically male profession, engineering, I note that ironically, the jobs centered around caring for others are the lowest paid, and are typically performed by women.

Work is challenging in that way, and so are romantic relationships. I want to be an equal partner in a romantic pairing. I do not want to be someone's assistant in our love relationship."

More of the people attending the class shared their stories and gave their opinions about the others' stories. When Aphrodite read the reviews for that class, many attendees shared that they had an increased awareness of what selfishness means, and they no longer confused it with self-care, although the line between the two is not always that clear. The class participants recognized that you do not have to be selfless, but that you have to have empathy in relationships, and to communicate face-to-face. For many, it was the beginning of the journey toward finding a more suitable mate, or working toward a better relationship in already established partnerships.

Aphrodite spoke with Rebecca about the class on selfishness during an individual therapy session. Rebecca reasoned that when it comes to behaving unselfishly in a relationship, there is no end to the daily communication effort required by both parties, and no end to her looking at her own behavior to see how she could improve and be empathetic toward her partner. She recognized, too, that she deserved the same effort from her future partner. It was not going to be easy.

Chapter Ten

Spoiled Brats Can Be Unspoiled

"Parents can only give good advice or put them on the right paths, but the final forming of a person's character lies in their own hands."

—Anne Frank

"A spoiled son becomes a gambler, while a spoiled daughter becomes a harlot."

—Anonymous

Marilyn was at wit's end. Her son Eric, who was forty-five years old, contacted her to ask for money, yet again. But that call had an added kicker. He wanted to move back into her home. Eric would work for a year or two, lose his job, stay out of work for another year or two studying something new, and then work for a while until another 'crisis' happened. He never thought the jobs were good enough for him. He disrespected his bosses. He worked less than his coworkers and had issues getting along with them. He chose to work for unstable companies without much of a track record. It was everyone else's fault that his employment was erratic. He jumped from career to career. He was terminally unhappy whether he was employed or not.

This pattern had been going on since he graduated college, which took him five years to complete instead of four, all paid for by his parents. He graduated college without any debt.

After marrying at age thirty-five, his wife divorced him two years later. He had one child with her whom he failed to support regularly. He was continually being taken to Family Court by his ex-wife to pay child support. He would ask Marilyn, frequently, to bail him out of his responsibility. A few times he was held in contempt for not paying, and Marilyn literally had to rescue him from his jail cell by providing the money he owed. When he had visitation with his child, he would often ask Marilyn to join them so that she could do the babysitting, and he could do what he wanted with that time.

I was a financial advisor with advanced degrees in psychology who specialized in issues regarding adult children. When I first met with Marilyn, she told me she was a retired widow, she had some money from her husband's estate, and she did sporadic part-time work to keep her busy and for a little extra cash. She was worried that Eric would drain her of all of her money and that she would not be able to take care of herself. She needed a plan.

Marilyn was desperate for Eric to become independent. She felt responsible for having created a "monster" and she needed help to get them both to a better place. He was emotionally abusive toward her, and blamed Marilyn for all of his own shortcomings. He would stop talking to her, or yell at her, or call her names if he did not get what he wanted. He would threaten to withhold visits with her granddaughter. What was perhaps his greatest manipulation, on multiple occasions throughout the years, he made veiled threats to harm himself if Marilyn did not help him. He had been using his "fragility" and "mental illness" as a manipulation to get money from his parents for years. Now that her husband died, it was all on her. Eric refused to take care of himself or his child, and that refusal manifested itself in a myriad of ways.

Marilyn sought my help to give her tools, and a plan, to cope emotionally and financially with what had become a problem without end. She felt that the stress from her son would kill her long before her son would do anything to himself. Her son had been in therapy since childhood, much of which she had paid for. She felt that he had the emotional support he needed, and would have to continue to work things through with his therapist.

I asked her why she thought that Eric turned out the way he did. She said that part of it was his innate temperament. He was difficult, in her view, from the moment he was born. He grew up to be a child who lacked empathy, and was always self-centered. She admitted to me that she and her now deceased husband had indulged Eric when he was a boy, and the spoiling never stopped. She had no problem taking ownership of how her parenting may have contributed to the problem, as she herself had a therapist who worked on that issue with her.

Awareness was a major first step. She explained:

"Eric's father, Thomas, and I came from humble beginnings. My husband became a successful businessman. I was a Professor of Physics at a respected college. Our parents were poor, and we had to work hard and struggle for everything. We had ambition to burn. We did not want Eric to suffer at all, and we wanted to give him everything we did not have. We continually encouraged him and told him that he could do whatever he wanted to do in life.

We did not give him chores or responsibilities because we had to work so hard when we were children. We wanted him to have it easier. We gave him few rules or schedules to govern his behavior. I felt guilty because I worked a lot, as did my husband, and so we would lavish him with time and assistance when we could, and we gave him too many material possessions. Eric ran our household from an early age.

Thomas, as a businessman, talked to Eric about values and money. Words without supporting actions did not work. Thomas gave Eric an allowance, but if Eric spent it all before his next payment, which happened frequently, Thomas did not make him wait to get more money. We never required Eric to do anything for that money. We did not adequately teach him that you cannot have or do everything you want and that there are trade-offs. We gave him instant gratification, and, consequently, Eric never learned patience or self-control.

Eric was rarely if ever grateful for what he was given. He always wanted more, and he was not generous with his friends. He had a hard time sharing. Many of his peers and adults distanced themselves from him because of his attitude. Even though we showed Eric that we gave money to charities, and that we did volunteer community work, he always balked at having to do so himself. We talked about how we helped other people. He was never interested in doing so, and we did not hold him to it. He would take on a volunteer job for a few weeks, and then his commitment would wane and he would stop participating.

We asked that he get paying jobs while he was in high school and college for spending money. He would obtain a job, hold it for a few weeks or months, and then either quit or get fired because he did not have work ethic or grit. He spoke back to his bosses and was insubordinate. He always wanted to start at the top of the ladder, and never wanted to do the 'dirty work.' We did not cut off his allowance, although we should have. He was raised to think he had it all coming to him. We did not hold him accountable enough.

Although Eric, as an adult, would try to make us feel guilty that we did not spend time with him when he was growing up, as he could sense that was a hot button for him to press, the truth is that we spent every weekend driving him around to his different activities, and we took him on every vacation we went on, which was not healthy for our marriage. Eric had a difficult time sustaining friendships with his peers, so he overly relied on us for company. Since Eric had such entitled behavior, as he grew up, few girls wanted to date him, and if they did, they would quickly break up with him. His guy friends grew tired of his selfish behaviors. He would blame all of them and us for his ending up lonely and alone, and refused to see how he had any part in what happened to him. What is sad is that he is intelligent, good looking, and had and has so much potential.

We sent Eric for therapy at an early age because of his difficulties functioning in school, at home, and with his friends. He refused to work hard, to do his best, to share with others or be part of a team. He was disrespectful to us, and our friends and relatives referred to him as a 'brat.' He became impossible to live with as he had grown constantly unhappy and insatiable.

His therapist worked with us, too, on teaching him delayed gratification, proper manners, respect for his elders, generosity and self-control. We tried to give less and expect more, but when Eric would have a tantrum, we eventually gave in. That tantrum looked different as he aged, but it was a tantrum nonetheless. He knew that if he cried, in one form or another, we would cave. We could not bear to see him suffer. We were at fault for not saying no more often, and for failing to give him structure and discipline.

When Eric was younger, he would whine, complain endlessly, and demand more and more. He would scream in public until he got his way. We had to continually battle for his cooperation, and he managed to create havoc in our household. Eric created a strain in our marriage, although we were able to withstand that assault. He would try to manipulate me against my husband, and vice versa. When he realized that divide and conquer did not work, he stopped trying that. Eric was a bright boy. He knew that if he acted out, he had a chance to get what he wanted. He would seek attention by getting bad grades and getting into trouble at school. Eric used drugs and alcohol as a teenager. He would seek revenge by not speaking with us. He would act helpless if that would get him what he wanted. Eric wanted to gain power and control at all times, and we let him have the power.

We had, and I am still having, the same conversation with him about being responsible now that he is middle-aged. We should have disciplined him by using consequences. We should have taught him that with privileges comes responsibilities. Instead, we were tired from work, and would give in and surrender. If Eric became frustrated, which he did easily, he would try to manipulate us by telling us we were bad parents, or that we did not love him. No matter how much we did for him, he would not do much in return. We flattered him, rewarded him when he did not deserve it, and fixed his mistakes. Perhaps we prevented him from developing life skills, and now he is greedy and dependent, far beyond the age when it would be remotely appropriate."

I asked her why they let the situation with Eric go on for so long. She said:

"Our biggest fear was that he would become angry with us and withhold love, which he did many times to control us. It was important to us, perhaps overly so, that Eric like us. Our other fears were that he would not be able to succeed on his own, and that somehow it was our fault because we did not do a good job as parents.

I know that I am repeating myself, but I become emotional when I speak about Eric, and I need to let the thoughts and feelings flow out of me, if you do not mind. I can honestly say that I felt tyrannized by him throughout his childhood into adulthood. We made things so easy for him, he never developed a thick enough skin to deal with difficulties in life. For many years as an adult, he has shown himself to be unable to manage the responsibilities, restraints and hardships of adulthood. He is prone to anxiety, depression, and troubled relationships, as the experts say happens to overindulged children. The world does not want to put up with his behaving in a self-centered, demanding, lazy and disrespectful way. When his wife left him, she told me that she could no longer live with someone so entitled.

Eric is tuned into my weaknesses. He plays to my guilt when I do not give him what he wants. As an adult, he self medicates with alcohol and drugs and is promiscuous because he cannot cope with the normal ups and downs of adult life, and then it compounds his problems with his underachievement. He acts like a minor child and makes me feel that he cannot live without my help and support. He makes many choices based on the moment without regard for future consequences.

I have so many fears for Eric. I worry about what will happen to him. He has a high standard of living because he grew up with wealthy peers. He has never been able to provide that for himself and cannot settle for less. I worry that he will hurt others emotionally, especially my grandchild. I worry that he will get a sexually transmitted disease because of his habits, and that he will knowingly pass it on to others. I feel sorry for him so I give into his demands. Most of all I am exhausted from being a prisoner on his roller coaster. Every time I think he is finally going to become independent, he finds a way to sabotage it and expresses an even greater need for me to show him my love by giving to him financially, and by making unreasonable demands for his age. He has made a full-time job of earning income from me by manipulating my emotions.

One of his biggest tricks is to hold out hope. He will say that if I just give him a sum of money for something, such as to take new courses, or to pay for his transportation, or to pay for this therapy, or to allow him a vacation to get into a better headspace, he will be able to succeed in whatever new venture he planned. Either he does not finish the course, or he takes the course but then decides he does not like the field, or he gets a job in the field and does not take to it, or he dislikes his employer and gets fired, and on and on. He begs me not to make him work. He gets angry with me if I say he has to.

Although I love him, I have to acknowledge that Eric is an angry, bitter person. He feels justified in his anger because he thinks that nobody treated him the way that they should have, including his parents. He is cynical with other people, and is overly critical. The other side of that equation is that he harbors a deep sense of shame, and a lot of insecurity about his abilities and about who he is as a person. Again I am repeating myself. When Eric does not get what he wants with overly aggressive behavior, he engages in attention-seeking behaviors coupled with self-pity. I know that he craves to be admired and adored, but his qualities prevent him from achieving that as everyone keeps a guarded distance.

Eric never asks me if I am o.k., or about my health, or if I have enough money. He never pays attention to my needs or those of others. He is unable to forgive people. Eric is unaware of other people's feelings. He is stuck in the mind-set of a self-absorbed teen, even at forty-five years of age. Eric has no sense of reciprocity. My son rarely if ever buys me a gift for my birthday. He insults the gifts I give to him. Eric never thinks about how his demands might impact me. He never offers to help me around my house or to do errands for me, even though I am elderly and alone. Given my age, and his, it is amazing.

Eric has a distant relationship with his child. He lets his ex-wife do all the parenting. He cancels visitation dates, or he shows up late and leaves early. My son is not attuned to his child's needs and does not seem to enjoy spending time with her. When I speak to him about it, he says that I was an absentee parent, so I have no right to criticize him.

What do I do now about this entitlement 'monster?' I fear that he does not have the skills to succeed nor a desire to develop them. I cannot hand him a great job or a stable relationship. I cannot make him a good father. Without his own focus, drive and dedication, he cannot achieve his own success. I need for my money to last me until I die, and because I have no real health issues, there are potentially many years ahead. Where do I draw the line between helping, enabling, and disabling him? My therapist and I have analyzed this together endlessly, but I need to take action now."

We talked about allowing adult children to struggle in order to find the key to their own lifelong success. We talked about the important lessons that Eric never learned: to be on time, to do what he says, to finish what he started, to do more than what is expected, and to maintain a great attitude. We discussed how she needed to stop caretaking, and just care for Eric. We spent time looking at how she parented out of emotion. We talked further about Marilyn's emotional buttons which moved her into a caretaking mode.

We discussed that she could not control her son's behavior, including his bouncing from career to career, but she could support him in his ability to make good decisions, and not support him financially if he failed to. This would make him responsible for the outcomes. She knew that unearned wealth retards ambition, as it had in her son's case She recognized that she needed to react with a well-considered response instead of purely reacting. The time was well overdue, by decades and decades, in fact.

After a number of sessions, we worked out a plan for Marilyn. I had many clients with significant portfolios who had adult children whom they were unwillingly supporting to everybody's detriment. I told her that she did not need Eric's permission to change how she was handling things, and to expect that his behavior would get worse before it would get better.

She decided to tell Eric that she would not allow him to move in with her. She knew that it would not be healthy for either of them. Once she finally had that conversation with Eric, he stopped speaking to her for one month.

She stopped giving him money. It was time to teach him about earning his own way, and about making himself happy through his own actions. She knew that she would have to set firm boundaries and limits. She worked out visitation with her grandchild through his ex-wife so that he could not use withholding that contact as a manipulation to get what he wanted.

After a month, he contacted her and asked if she would pay the downpayment for him to purchase a two-bedroom apartment, and to co-sign the papers for the mortgage. He insisted that he needed a two-bedroom apartment in case his child came to visit. He told her that he should have that size apartment, also, because she had two bedrooms, and he should not have anything less than she had. Marilyn said no as she was retired and needed her savings for her own retirement. She also said that until he had stable employment for many years, he would not be able to pay the mortgage and maintenance on his own, so it was not practical. He told her that all of his childhood friends owned their own apartments, and that their parents helped them out. She still said no. He cried, and then stopped talking to her for a few more months.

Then she received a telephone call from Eric. He said that he needed money to pay for bariatric surgery as it was his weight that was interfering with his employment. He said that people fat shamed him, that he was discriminated against at work, and that no women wanted to date him. She said no, and supported him with information about appropriate diets and told him to make healthier food choices. Eric told Marilyn that she was a terrible mother, that all his problems were because of her, and that she did not love him or she would help him to improve his appearance.

He ranted that he always loved his father more, and if he were alive, he would have helped him. He screamed at her and accused her of being selfish and of spending inordinate amounts of money on herself since she owned her own large apartment, had a cleaning lady once per week, and had her hair dyed at a beauty salon. He listed all of the ways in which she spent money on herself. He accused her of being narcissistic and mean. She explained to him that she and his father had worked all of their lives, had saved money to live on in their old age, and that she was entitled to a comfortable retirement.

When she stopped giving him money, he started to ask her, each time they spoke, about what he would be getting in her will. It made her feel as though he would be happier if she was dead. He had already burned through the money his father left him in his will.

Marilyn thought that with her having said no to all of these different unreasonable demands, and with her fair and sensible explanations, Eric would stop asking her for money, and would stop blaming her for everything which went wrong in his life. She should have known better. When they met to talk every few months, he would tell her his hard luck stories so that she would feel sorry for him, and there was frequently an ask for money, or something Marilyn needed to do for him, tied in with the visit. If there was no ask for money, he berated her.

Usually he did both.

A year later Eric contacted her, and said he had a job, but that they were going to lay people off. Several weeks later he asked her for money to pay for a course for a new venture, and to help him out with his car payments. She said no. She told him to look for a different job before he got fired, and to pay for the course himself. He threatened to harm himself. She e-mailed his therapist to warn him. Although the therapist would not speak with her, she felt she had done her best by letting him know.

A short time later, Eric told her about a business he wanted to start. He accused Marilyn of not trusting him when she refused to give him seed money. He told her that once he had the initial capital, he would pay her back. This time, when she refused, he cried and cried. She finally let him cry without feeling guilt.

Another time he told her that he had no friends, and needed her to take him on vacations and take him out to nice restaurants and cultural events, all paid by her. She told him that if he would treat people well, and be a better friend, he would have more friends, and that she wanted to travel with her own friends. She told him that he needed to be more independent. He again told her that she was a bad mother.

I did not hear from Marilyn for a few years. We had worked out a solid financial plan, and she was having no difficulty following it. She stopped letting Eric manipulate her, as difficult as that was. When she gave him advice about how to better handle his finances, he accused her of making him anxious and sicker, causing him to be paralyzed emotionally, in his words. The next time she contacted me, she told me all of that and more. She said that Eric was still seeing a therapist, that he was taking his medication, and that he was working. He visited with his daughter sporadically, and gave her little money. He lived alone, he had a few friends, and he continued to berate Marilyn.

Marilyn said that her son repeated the same accusations against her over and over again from his childhood, specifically that Marilyn did not spend enough time with him while he was growing up and that he was raised by nannies. It was a broken record. Eric repeatedly asked her to apologize for her parental 'sins'. When she apologized, which she was forced to do over and over by him, he did not accept what she said. She knew that he would never stop emotionally abusing her, but at least she felt confident that she could hold the line and do what she needed to do so that she could enjoy her golden years without becoming financially insolvent.

Many years later I heard from Marilyn again as we needed to make some minor adjustments to her financial plan. She told me that her granddaughter was extremely responsible, had put herself through college and graduate school with scholarships and loans, and had started working in a high paying job in the financial industry. Marilyn shared with me that Eric borrowed money from his own daughter, and that, she too, was having trouble saying no to him. Was I surprised? No.

Chapter Eleven

Does It Matter If Women And Men Grieve Differently?

"She was no longer wrestling with the grief, but could sit down with it as a lasting companion and make it a sharer in her thoughts."

—George Eliot

"Well, every one can master a grief but he that has it."

—William Shakespeare

Nancy and Gary's teenage son, Kenny, died at 1:00 a.m. when he was driving home alone from a party in the suburbs. The windy, narrow roads were dark and slick with rain. His car skidded and crashed headlong into a tree. It was later determined that Kenny's car had been traveling at an excessive rate of speed. The police went to his home several hours later, rang the doorbell, and gave his parents the news. The police were able to get their address from Kenny's license, which was in his wallet in his jeans. For a long time afterwards, the parents thought that they were dreaming, and then they wondered, "why us," and felt like abject failures.

When the autopsy was performed, it revealed that Kenny had drugs and alcohol in his system. None of the facts regarding the "reasons" for the accident were a comfort to Nancy and Gary. There were parts of Nancy and of Gary that both died with Kenny that night. They never found a reason they could live with for his early death.

Kenny was the youngest of four children. He was hard working, intelligent, and had the expressed ambition to become a doctor. After school, he worked at a local pharmacy, and volunteered at the community hospital. Kenny had a winning personality, a subtle sense of humor, a perpetual smile on his face, and a certain believable optimism which drew people to him. Ironically, he was not a big risk taker, and was not known to be someone who used alcohol and drugs excessively. He experimented, lightly, as many teenagers do. Unfortunately, the night he died was one of those nights of testing the limits.

His siblings were grown and lived elsewhere, but quickly returned home when they were told about his death. The day after the accident, the family sat around the living room, while Kenny's body was being prepared at the funeral home by the professionals there. There would be no open casket for Kenny as his face and body were beyond repair. People used to be born and died at home. Kenny was lying alone with strangers. The family felt disconnected from his death but feared seeing him in that state.

Ironically, Kenny's eldest sister, Sally, was a professional bereavement counselor. She helped with all of the arrangements, and delegated tasks to her siblings and to her husband. She created a collage of photographs of Kenny with their family. Gary and Nancy could not function, and sat quietly, staring into space. After the funeral, the burial, and the wake, which was experienced by all of them as a blur, Sally stayed with her parents to help them through the first month as she lived close by. She took a temporary leave from her job. Her husband returned to his job, and visited on the weekends. Sally took care of tasks around the home and managed their finances. After a time, she referred her parents to a colleague, Ann, who was also a bereavement counselor and worked with couples. Sally had her own grieving which she needed to do, and she needed to get back to her life.

Sally observed her parents going through the process of grief, and knew, from her professional experience, that they would never be the same again, nor would she. Parents are not supposed to outlive their children and the loss of a child is known to be one of the most stressful events that parents could experience in their lifetime. While she knew, intellectually, that the ways in which people cope with grief are all different, and that women and men often grieve differently, it was jarring to see it in her parents and herself.

Sally was aware that grief reactions after the loss of a child can often be more intense and last longer than with other deaths. She did not want her family to be torn apart due to their inability to understand each other's bereavement differences. Sally hoped that the family could get its equilibrium back and tried to protect her parents.

Gary was the true patriarch of his family. He was considered the dependable "rock" not only in his family, but also in his position as a manager at work, in his community, and with his male friends with whom he liked to watch and play sports and go hunting. He was never a person who showed too much emotion. Part of it was that he was afraid that if he let his feelings out, he might never be able to shut them off. The other part was that he had been suppressing his emotions for so long, he did not know how to express them. He was raised to be strong and stoic, as are many men.

After Kenny's death, Gary preferred to spend more time alone hiking in the woods, thinking. On the other end of the spectrum, Gary threw himself into his work, into domestic chores, and joined a rugby team. He started to build an addition on their house. By becoming involved in physical work, he tried to push down the pain. He began to drink more than he had before. He expressed anger, and initially blamed Kenny's friends for allowing him to get in his car and drive in his condition.

While Gary was grieving on the inside, and approaching his grief in a cognitive and physical way, Nancy was reaching out to her friends and family for emotional support, and was expressing her emotions. She was raised to be emotional and sensitive. She felt guilty that she had allowed Kenny to go out that night, and that she had not given him permission to extend his curfew, which is why he might have been speeding. She blamed herself for his death. She faulted herself for failing to keep him safe and protected, which was her job.

Gary had a difficult time watching Nancy cry every day, and seeing her withdraw into a fetal position on their bed, or spend hours sobbing on the telephone while talking with her best girlfriends. He did not know how to handle it. She was having a tough time functioning physically and emotionally. She did not believe that she would ever be able to experience happiness again. She suffered from debilitating headaches and stomach cramps. Nancy was unable to understand Gary's inability to cry in front of anyone, and resented his spending a lot of time away from home. She felt that he was running away from his grief and pulling away from her just when she needed him most. She could not relate to his disconnecting his head from his heart. She wanted his support, and did not feel she was getting it. Gary's grief manifested itself differently. It impacted his health such that he developed an irregular heartbeat for which he had to be treated. Neither of them could eat or sleep well. Nancy was scared to drive, and became anxious when other family members drove.

When Gary and Nancy went to the bereavement counselor, named Ann, she explained to them that while she did not prefer to categorize grief, there are some patterns that are considered masculine or feminine ways of reacting to grief, and that they fell somewhat classically into those patterns. Nancy had what was termed intuitive grief and Gary had what was called instrumental grief. When they told Ann about how Sally was dealing with the loss, Ann said that Sally, on the other hand, was a blended griever in that she expressed her emotions, but also threw herself into task-oriented behaviors. Ann said that people grieve as they live, so that if one is emotional or stoic, one will be emotional or stoic in grief.

Ann told them that she wanted to give them a safe place to discuss their feelings. Over many months, they endured agonizing sessions. Nancy said that she was having difficulty relating to the way in which Gary was processing his grief. She said that he refused to talk about Kenny or his feelings about Kenny's death. Nancy felt that Gary wanted to move forward with his life, and in doing so, was leaving her behind. She felt that he was getting himself too busy with work, chores and other activities, and that their couple life was suffering. She felt isolated and alone in their marriage, and was angry with him that he would not work through the grief with her. She wanted to feel the pain and he did not. She did not want to forget

Kenny, and felt guilty about what happened to him. Nancy felt that by talking about Kenny, they were keeping his memory alive. She concluded that perhaps Gary loved Kenny less.

Gary said that he needed to feel accepted for the way in which he wanted to process grief, even if it was different from the way Nancy experienced it, and asserted that there was no right way to grieve. He said that he loved Kenny every bit as much as she did. Gary maintained that he thought that it was positive that Nancy had a social network of friends to discuss her feelings with, and that they both had Sally to talk with, as well as their other children. He confessed that he was afraid that he would say or do the wrong thing when talking with Nancy, which would make Nancy even sadder. Gary expressed that he was trying to distract himself with activities, and to "fix" things literally and figuratively, but that perhaps he could do an activity with Nancy so that she would not feel abandoned. He felt responsible to take control of the family needs, but said that he could understand how his absence made Nancy feel.

He articulated that Nancy kept repeating the same stories over and over again to process her feelings, but that made him feel uncomfortable. Gary felt that he could not get over the loss if they kept talking about their thoughts and feelings. He did not understand how to best support her without losing more of himself. He felt abandoned by Nancy in his own way in that she did not want to have sex because she was so depressed. He needed physical contact.

Nancy said that she was beginning to understand that he had a quieter, less visible way of grieving, and that his mode of healing was to connect to the future with an action plan. She realized that she had to accept and respect his style of healing. She suggested that perhaps they could set up a memorial fund together in Kenny's honor which would allow her to remember him, and would enable Gary to become involved in an action plan which would satisfy both of their needs. She said that she was not rejecting Gary when she did not want to have sex, but was not feeling sexual. Her grief had taken away her sex drive. She realized that she had to work on that aspect of their lives so that they could comfortably support one another.

Both Gary and Nancy shared that they both felt shocked and confused when the police officers told them that Kenny had died in an accident. They both had trouble, initially, handling daily tasks, such that Sally had to take over for a while. They recognized that they both felt guilty in their own ways for what had happened, and both felt that they should have done something more to protect Kenny. They acknowledged that they both felt angry and bitter that they had to lose a child, and were resentful at times toward parents who did not have to suffer such a loss. They admitted to one another that while neither was suicidal, they both felt, initially, that life had no meaning and that they wished, on some level, to join their child. Recognizing all of the feelings that they shared helped Nancy to realize that Gary was moving with her through grief, and by not expressing his own grief as much, he was leaving room for her to express her grief.

They talked about the fact that certain friends had been supportive in a way they could not have imagined, while other friends did not know what to say, and withdrew from them. They acknowledged that they had both experienced secondary losses of people they could no longer relate to after their loss. Nancy expressed that she lost the ability to engage in "small talk" for the longest time, and had no patience for friends who complained about things she no longer thought were significant. She lost friends who were frustrated over her inability to "get over the loss," or who avoided talking about Kenny. Gary admitted that he felt isolated in his loss from his friends and coworkers at times.

Nancy said that she believed she had seen Kenny in her dreams, and in shadows in his room and elsewhere. She talked to him in her sleep and while she was awake, and told him how she felt guilty for surviving while he died. She claimed that Kenny told her that it was not her fault, that it was his mistake, but that he is happy where he is. Nancy chose to believe that there is an afterlife, and that death is not just an end without meaning. Gary related that he had not experienced seeing Kenny after his death, and acknowledged that Nancy is a constant reminder of Kenny, but not in a bad way.

They stayed in therapy together for two years. Neither was finished grieving, but they felt that they had achieved what they could from therapy. When they reached milestones in the lives of other children such as graduations and weddings, they felt intense grief as before. Grief came in waves, with no rules or timetables. It had its own momentum. The grieving was never completely over, but they had learned to live with the loss, and made it part of themselves.

Sometimes the grief was in the back of their minds, and sometimes it was in the forefront, and not necessarily at the same time for each of them. While they adapted to the pain and gradually accepted the loss, the loss was irreversible and their functioning would never be the same.

Their marriage lasted because they worked on it, and because they had hope for their marriage. The therapy helped them both to overcome their depression and other problems relating to their loss, their feelings of anger, guilt and blame, and any marital dissatisfaction they felt. They knew and were prepared for the fact that Kenny's birthday and other milestones would trigger a period of heightened grief in what they came to understand as the circular grief process. They developed a deeper bond after their loss, and, with the help of their therapist, rediscovered their marriage. Kenny had been their youngest and only child living in their home when he died, and now they made more time for one another, and tuned into each other's needs more completely.

The family as a whole worked together as a supportive unit and regained their stability. They talked about Kenny, and used his name often. Each year, on the anniversary of Kenny's death, the entire family came together and planted flowers in a garden they created at Gary and Nancy's house, which was the home where the children grew up. Nancy felt Kenny's presence there every year. Sally did too. Gary was not able to experience that Kenny was with them, but he glowed with love to be surrounded by his loving wife, children and grandchildren.

Acknowledgements

I wrote this book before and during the coronavirus pandemic as I sat in its epicenter in New York City, sheltered at home. I had been reflecting on endings in all of these short stories, and none seemed as hard to fathom as reality. How will our lives ultimately be shaped, surprisingly, and not so surprisingly, by this disease? How will it all end? Many lost their lives. What will happen to those of us who remain? The answers are not yet in as of this writing.

Thank you to my now fourth time editor, Rae Ellen Vitiello, for her helpful comments, and to my life partner, Amos Grunebaum, for reading through my drafts and giving his always insightful comments. And, finally, thank you to Adelaide Publishing for continuing to believe in my work.

About the Author

Susan L. Pollet lives in New York City, and has been an attorney for over forty years, primarily in the area of family law. She has published over sixty articles on varied legal topics, including family and criminal law. She is also a published author and artist. In 2019, her first novel LESSONS IN SURVIVAL: ALL ABOUT AMOS was published by Adelaide Books. She created the collage for the book cover. Three of her short stories were published by Adelaide Literary Magazine in 2019, 2020 and 2021, respectively. In 2020, her second and third novels, THROUGH WALTER'S LENS and WOMEN IN CRISIS: STORIES FROM THE EDGE, were published by Adelaide Books. She painted the images for the book covers for those books as well. Her first children's book, entitled ON

BECOMING JULIETTE ROSE, with her text and illustrations, was published by Adelaide in the fall of 2020. Her fourth novel, A GREY DIVORCE SUPPORT GROUP, was published by Adelaide Books in 2021. She created the book cover.

www.ingramcontent.com/pod-product-compliance
Lightning Source LLC
Chambersburg PA
CBHW030636190726
48286CB00008B/2544